First, do no harm

Freya Kissane

ISBN: 978-0-9756629-0-8978-0-9756629-0-8
ISBN-13:

For the girl,
I was before.

1

First

There's this question that used to roll around in my head a lot as a kid.

In the movie of your life who would play you?

When I was seven, this question was mostly about which actress your friends agreed was your celebrity lookalike. We never stopped to imagine what these movies would actually contain. What would happen in them.

Since I've been writing this book that question has come back to me a lot.

In the movie of your life who would play you?

But it's no longer just about who I look like.

Instead it's become more about who I would trust with every moment of my life. Who I would trust to do the important bits justice. Who I would trust to not make the scary bits look silly. Who I would trust to make you really feel the heartbreaking bits.

Trust is important here. This is a trust fall, me writing this story. I'm allowing myself to fall backwards without knowing if you will catch me. There's a chance I could end up with my head smacking hard against the concrete. Because there's a chance you won't care enough to break my fall. There's a chance you won't care enough to read on. That you will close the book or the app or the illegal free ebook website and go on with your life.

I don't want to waste your time. I know that there are other things you could be doing now. You could spend this time learning to knit. Or to waterski. You could be learning how to trade stocks. Or be taking a nap.

And I know that the words on these pages are always going to feel more important to me than they will to you.

I wrestled a lot with the best way to tell this story. What to put in? What to leave out? Whether to name names? Whether to write my own name? Whether to tell it at all? Whether it would be better left alone? Left to sit safely in a vault in my mind, one that I rarely ever open.

First, they tell you start with a why. A why. A reason why you're doing this. At least, that seems to be the consensus of the YouTube productivity rabbit hole I sometimes dive into when I'm struggling to write.

You must have a why, otherwise there's no way in hell you'll follow through.

So why, April? Why are you writing this book?

Because no one will tell this story if I don't.

And you, why should you read this book?

Because this is a story that deserves to be read.

2

Two Part Obsession

At fourteen, my life revolved around a set schedule of predictable rhythms, that were rarely disrupted. I went to school and came home with homework. I took exams. I hung out with friends. I brushed my teeth twice a day. Life was in a word, simple.

In every possible way, my life was completely ordinary. People are the sum of their choices, but at fourteen most of the significant ones are still undecided, waiting to be made, cornered off in an unmarked file labelled 'The Future.'

The first thing that truly took over my life came as a package deal. A combination of figure skating and a boy who played ice hockey.

I'd started skating late, at the ripe old age of eleven, far too late to ever catch up to the kids that were my age. I spent years taking lessons once a week in group classes where everyone else was four years my junior. Nothing about skating came easily to me. Every new skill was a long drawn out battle to master. Almost every session involved sore muscles and large bruises.

Perhaps the draw of it was the difficulty, the struggle, that everything felt nearly impossible, until I did it. I doubt if it had come easily to me I would have liked it as much. There was nothing in the world I found more gratifying, more rewarding than the hours I spent in ten degree temperatures under the high ceilings of the converted aircraft hanger that was now an ice rink. Training became like a religion to me. I spent every possible minute of my free time there, which of course is how I developed the second part of my obsession—Jake.

Jake was enviably good looking. He had twinkling blue eyes, an easy smile and light brown hair that just seemed to fall effortlessly into place. When I list his features like this, these qualities seem cheesy and entirely superficial but the infatuation of your first crush is rarely about character, humour, intelligence or any of the other things that become important to you later on. Teenage hormones are at terrible making any kind of assessment of compatibility.

The week Jake and his first girlfriend became Facebook official, I was learning my first spin. Spinning in figure skates is something that the body acclimatises to gradually. In the beginning, the world seems to tilt at weird angles and it takes you a minute or so between attempts to see straight again but with practice you stop feeling dizzy almost entirely. The world rotates in circles around you and your head remains clear. You can turn in tight circles without anything shifting, without the world tilting in multiple directions. In the same way as my head got used to the centripetal force of spinning, my heart got used to the feelings brought on by an unrequited love. My head was full of visions of what the real thing would feel like, I scripted deep and meaningful conversations that took place between us. I watched as weeks and then months went by, as one of his relationships ended and another began and I waited for it to be my turn.

The small figure skating competitions I began to do also involved a sort of waiting game. There was always a gap, an in-between time, after getting off the ice following the minute warm-up and waiting for when I would get back on the ice to perform my program.

'Walk, keep walking, don't you dare get cold,' I can still hear the instructions barked by another coach to her nine-year-old student.

I knew I stood out in this group of eight and nine-year-olds milling around the stretch of rubber matting between the barrier of the ice rink and the stands. I couldn't help it. I was almost double their age. I tried not to let the humiliation of that sting too deeply. Tried to remind myself it didn't matter that the girls my age were all landing double jumps, while I was still struggling with singles. I tried being my own personal self-help guru and quoting mantras to myself like 'You are on your own journey' and 'You will get there eventually.' But even in my head these words felt hollow. As a I stood in that huddle of petite little girls in short sparkly dresses and glittering eyeshadow, I knew I didn't want to be fourteen. It felt like a competition that I had already lost by being too late to the party.

Collectively, we were all trying not to the watch the girl who was currently on the ice. This was the only universally agreed upon piece of advice that all the coaches offered. It will only make you more nervous. Most of us were failing dismally at trying not to look. Even the girl been forced to power walk up and down the ten-metre stretch of rubber was sneaking glances at the ice.

There's a desperate urge that tugs in all of our minds, a deep yearning for the girl on the ice to make a mistake. Slip up in some small way, that somehow if she does, that will make it easier to wait, take the pressure off the rest of us. No one wants her to get hurt, but a fall wouldn't be the worst thing. Just a little fall. That's all.

The girl on the ice was spinning. I watched her rise from a

sit position and shift her weight to the other foot pulling into a fast back spin. Her tiny yellow dress rippled around her, the music swelled and then stopped. She held her final position smiling at the judges. Scattered applause echoed from the stands, which were never full. I watched her skate back to the barrier gate, a satisfied smile on her face.

I felt a light pressure on my back as my coach prodded me forward towards the gate. I was next. I stepped onto the ice as the girl in the yellow dress stepped off. There was still more waiting though. The judges are reviewing their scores before posting them. I turned away from them and looked at my coach. She reached for both my hands over the edge of the barrier.

The speaker system crackled to life. The announcer said my name.

My coach squeezed my hands, 'Tell me a story,' she said as she released them.

The words echoed in my head as I held my first position, then the music started.

I remember the song that was playing when I got to the party wasn't one that I recognised. As I was greeted with hugs and loud exclamations of 'April!' and 'April's here,' I was almost tempted to ask who the artist is, but I don't want to seem uncool in the presence of my brand new skating friends, who were all actually born in the same decade as me. I felt lucky to be there. Lucky to be invited. I knew them, but not in the real way you know someone. I knew them from having watched them talk to each other, from having scrolled through Facebook profiles and from being on the edges of conversations. As a result the aura of cool I'd coated them with was thick enough to make me awkward and nervous.

This was the first house party that I'd ever really wanted to go to. Even though at least in theory, I felt like an expert.

There was a house in my street, two houses down from mine, where older kids from private schools had been gathering to throw house parties since we moved in. I don't think anyone actually ever lived there during the week. But without fail, every Friday or Saturday since we had moved in there had been some kind of house party. I had watched those parties from my bedroom window, gradually becoming fascinated by the kids that went to them.

None of my carefully catalogued research seemed to apply to this party though. The music was quieter. There were less people, even for 9pm. Everyone knew each other. There was also a themed dress code. Black and white. Almost everyone had stuck to it too. I tried to imagine the house parties on my street being like this. This sedate, everyone following the rules the host had laid out. I couldn't ever see it happening.

As the night progressed, I slipped into my favourite habit in any social situation, people watching. I tried not to watch Jake and his current girlfriend, but I couldn't really help myself. They weren't sitting with the main group, who were playing a drinking game. They spent most of the night, out on the balcony at the back of the house. I couldn't hear the conversation, so I had to content myself with the body language. Neither of them looked particularly thrilled with the other. It seemed like she was trying to get him to stay with her out on the balcony, and he wanted to return to the main group inside. This tug of war between them was brief, I doubt anyone else even noticed it but it made me unreasonably gleeful. My unrequited pinning for Jake had created a paradoxical state where I yo-yoed between my commitment to the mantra that 'if she makes him happy that makes me happy' and simultaneously watched the relationship like a hawk for signs of trouble and distress, the same way an overeager lifeguard watches a pool on summer afternoon.

As I watched their body language and saw the fault lines of a breakup emerging, I tried to push down my delight and remind myself of my philosophy that loving someone without needing them to return it is real love.

Still, when they started saying goodbye to people and headed towards the street to wait for the parental taxi service home that we were all still bound by at that point, I texted my own mother, 'Ready for pick-up.' The excuse to walk past on the quiet laneway that led to the house, where they would both be forced to acknowledge me was too tempting to miss.

They were leaned against a low brick wall, I planned to walk past with a small wave and maybe a mumbled goodnight but as I approached Jake turned towards me. He opened his arms as though summoning me for a hug. I blushed instantly. It was so public, right in front of his very much real, very much now annoyed girlfriend.

I smiled and made a joke of walking past. His face dropped. He looked genuinely hurt. I stopped, I couldn't deny myself this. Friends could hug. It didn't have to mean anything. He was just being a friend, I told myself.

So, I stepped into the embrace. Time seemed to slow down at my request. Like someone knew I really wanted to make that moment last. It felt more romantic, standing there in his arms than a lot of kisses I've had since. The feeling of his hands on my waist seemed to say, 'Wait for me, April. I want it to be you.'

I know now that I held onto that small moment for years longer than I should have. In spite of mounting evidence that it would never really be my turn, I kept hoping.

Neither skating or Jake would have become such fixtures in my life, if they'd been easy to obtain. For a long time, they were hard to separate. They were the same dream wrapped together.

I don't think letting go is ever as simple as Elsa makes it

out to be. The distance of time makes most things seem smaller than they were in our youth. A veneer of glitter and giddiness floats away and you're left with the realisation that most love is embarrassing. Nothing about letting go ever happens on a reasonable timeline but you can't rush it. It's always easier to choose to let go of something, when you're finally ready than to have it ripped out of your hands.

3

Snakes and Pebbles

This part of my story takes place on a Thursday. A Thursday, that I thought at the time had to be the worst day of my life. Then, I could not imagine a worse day ever occurring.

I remember as I was walking out of my last class, I checked my watch. It was 3:12 pm. Much later than I would've liked. I was already late in my race to exit the school grounds as fast as possible. On my way back to homeroom, I rounded a corner on a path between buildings and almost ran directly into another student.

From the oversized bag and the tunic that almost reached her ankles, I knew she was a year seven. I could also tell she was nearly in tears, which she rapidly tried to hide as she saw me. I didn't want to stop. My stride faltered in a moment of indecision. Then, I reminded myself I'm not the kind of person who walks away from a crying 11-year-old. I was already dreading the answer as I asked her what's wrong. She swallowed and tried to speak.

'I was asking Evil Science Teacher a question that I got wrong and... and... It was weird. I don't know to how to explain...' She dissolved into tears and hiccups.

I reached gently for her shoulders. It's okay, I heard myself say, I understand.

Evil Science Teacher is the kind of person I hate most in this world — a snake — a snake that hides in a beautiful garden. Because for the most part my school is the kind of school you want your child to attend. The teachers are well educated, passionate and caring. They're the kind of people who believe teaching the next generation will make the world a better place. Evil Science Teacher is the only exception. He's the one rotten apple.

Evil Science Teacher always got a class of year seven students, and informed them that he was there should they have any questions about homework or exams. Come and see me after class, any time, he proclaimed, stressing the 'any time'. I wasn't sure if evil science teacher even liked science. Maybe at one point he did. But I suspected any passion that he had ever had, had shifted a long time ago. I suspected the only thing he liked about his job now was little girls. But the brand new 11-year-olds with their full pencil cases, bright ambitious minds and happy sheltered childhoods didn't know this. So it made sense, that when they didn't understand why they had lost half a mark on question seven, they'd go to Evil Science Teacher.

And all this would have been fine, except it stopped being fine the moment Evil Science Teacher put his hand on their knee.

Behind the junior homerooms is an area they called the peace garden. It was a curving path of white pebbles that led to a fishpond with big orange koi fish. It's here that I took the girl, whose name I've only just learned. To sit on a bench in this quiet, peaceful secret garden. I didn't ask her to tell me what happened, I didn't need to. I just tried and find the right words. The words that would comfort her.

First I said that she shouldn't go and see Evil Science Teacher again. That she shouldn't worry about science this year. I told her that nothing that happened this afternoon was right or okay and she shouldn't have to hold it. Or hold onto it. Then I told her to pick up a pebble from the ground, and to place everything she was feeling inside the pebble and then to throw it into the pond. Let it go. Don't carry it with you. Leave it there at the bottom of the pond.

We sat there for a few more minutes before she was ready to throw the pebble into the pond. It filled me with an overwhelming heaviness sitting there with her. I am reminded of the end of my first week of year seven, three years ago, when I sat in my own ill-fitting tunic with a girl in my own year, I hadn't met before that day, who also had the misfortune to have Evil Science Teacher that year.

It was that afternoon, when I was 11 that I first learned that justice and healing weren't necessarily the same thing. If karma worked, or justice was something the universe believed in, then Evil Science Teacher would have been burned to a crisp where he stood a long time ago. But that kind of justice isn't something that really exists. And it wouldn't necessarily have helped the girl's that Evil Science Teacher hurt anyway.

You can argue the morality of the situation all day long, and go backwards and forwards about the right thing to do. But sometimes, the only thing you can have any impact on is how you treat the person in front of you, the one who is hurting. Sometimes the best thing you can do for someone who is hurting is to offer to hold their pain for them. To store it somewhere inside yourself so they don't have to carry it around with them.

As I was thinking this, the girl beside me, took a deep breath and threw the pebble into the pond.

'Better?' I asked.

'Yeah,' she said.

I checked my watch, 3.21pm, I should be in the bus line

already. After I parted ways with the year seven, I had a decision to make. I was meant to go to afternoon homeroom and get my name marked off. I didn't want to. As I walked down the stairs to Lab 1, I felt hot tears in my eyes. I remember thinking that history was always doomed to repeat itself. I was angry that in three years later nothing much had changed and I was doing the same service for a different girl.

I didn't know it that particular Thursday but I would spend many of my teenage years acting as a vault for other girl's painful memories. I became a collector of this particular type of story. I made folders on my computer with each of their names. Those girls whose secrets I kept. I wrote down accounts of what they told me, attaching any available evidence. After that, I would close the word doc and try to fill the folder with beautiful things. Pictures of sunsets, places to travel to, words about love and healing, anything I could find that I thought would make it less painful if anyone ever needed to open the folder. I didn't want the girls whose stories I carried just to see the world through the ugliness of what had happened to them.

As much as I tried to believe in beautiful things, I was learning that there was often a sick kind of humour in the way the universe works. Like needing one medication to counter the side effects of another. Or the way the bus will inevitably run late the one day you need to be early. Or the fact that Evil Science Teacher happened to be my homeroom teacher that year.

This meant that he was the last person I needed to see that day before I could escape the school grounds. The procedure of getting your name marked off for the afternoon homeroom involved stacking three stools in the science lab and then telling Evil Science Teacher which stools you had stacked.

I wasn't surprised when I entered that afternoon that only three stools remained unstacked. Or that Evil Science Teacher was standing at the back of the room next to those three stools.

I didn't like having to go this close to him. In truth, his energy repulsed me. I wanted to scream, How could you? You fucking monster.

But instead I made my way to the desk and reluctantly turned my back on him to put the stools up. There was so much anger in my body that my hands were shaking with the effort to keep it inside.

I think Evil Science Teacher might have even asked me if I was okay in his sickly crackling voice.

He didn't really care. We both knew that. It was fake showboat kind of compassion, not real kindness.

I responded with a Mhmm.

I'm not sure whether he put his hand on my leg that day or another day later that year, but I do remember it happened at some point.

I remember telling him to go right ahead, that I couldn't wait to report him. To watch him get fired. Go to prison. I remember him shrinking back from me as though my skin was made of acid.

4

Common Beasts

Snakes are common beasts in the worlds of teenage girls. They hide in all kinds of gardens. Sadly, Evil Science Teacher was not the only snake I would encounter that day.

There was one coach at the ice rink who had always made me uneasy. He was Russian, very good at teaching turns and step sequences, but there was something about him I just didn't like. He was the kind of coach who liked to make corrections by touching his students, manipulating their bodies into the correct positions, standing close enough that they could tell whether he'd brushed his teeth or not.

Kids with natural talent in figure skating are rare. The sport is such a mix of flexibility, strength and artistry, all demanded simultaneously, that most kids require a ton of coaching just to master basic skills with any proficiency.

Sadie was the closest thing I have ever seen to a natural. Her joy for the sport seemed to radiate through her and into everything she did on the ice. Sadie skated with a fluid, elegant water-like quality that seemed to come from a nebulous place that could not have existed inside the head of an eight-year-old, an imprint of a past life spent at a ballet barre during the day and nights walking a tightrope to incredulous applause. She was impressive to watch and she improved at a rate that exceeded even the most optimistic expectations. Coaches began pulling her parents to one side, asking for more lessons, an off-ice conditioning program and Gold Seal blades for her to skate on. There was an aura surrounding her skating. An aura that seemed to say this kid is going places.

When Sadie began taking lessons from this Russian Coach, I remember a sinking feeling in my stomach that something bad would happen. I took my unprovable fears to Sadie's mother and when that failed I made it my personal mission to skate every single session I possibly could and watch every lesson Sadie had with this coach.

This was where I was headed to after school that Thursday. Why I was impatient to get on the bus as fast as possible. I'd been watching these lessons for months, and although nothing had happened yet, I couldn't shake the uneasy feeling that I was watching a child being groomed.

It was that Thursday that the Russian Coach decided to tell Sadie to go into the bathroom during her lesson and I watched him glance around the rink, jump off the ice and follow after her.

In that moment I knew I had another choice. I could stay anxiously at the edge of the barrier and wait for it to be over. Or I could run in there and try to stop what I was almost sure I knew was happening. Everything I knew from my own childhood told me that if it was allowed to happen today it would keep happening. That fact alone was scarier than entering the bathroom, so I got off the ice and ran the few steps to the toilets. The sight that greeted me was not a pleasant one.

Sadie's clothes were scattered around the floor, she was shivering in her panties, and the Russian coach had his erect penis out and was encouraging her to touch it. That was when I screamed at him to get away from her and get out. I remember being conscious of the fact that I didn't really have a plan if he didn't comply with my demands and tried to hurt me, but he fled at a lightning pace.

The next bit took considerably more time. I sat down in the bathroom and for the second time that day tried to find the right words for the confused and scared kid in front of me. The first thing I did was give her my jacket to wear and then I began to document the scene. I explained what I was doing and why and asked for her permission to take photos and did my best to document the small amount of evidence in the grimy bathroom. I then sat with Sadie and explained what had happened to her. I explained the process of grooming as I understood it, and I asked her to tell me what had happened, which I recorded for evidence.

Then I spoke to Sadie's Mum. I advised her to take her daughter home and put her in a bubble bath and to make her favourite dinner. I told her that when my mother had been faced with a similar situation, she had let it harden her. Turn her into a lioness. I told her what was needed was softness. Gentleness. A purring house cat. Then together with the staff, I wrote an account of what I'd seen, signed it and went home.

Here, a wave of hopelessness overwhelmed me. The world was a sick, twisted place full of cruelty and nastiness. I bawled my eyes out in the shower. It wasn't something I could tell my parents about. That would only drag up the remains of past hurt, force them to relive one of the most difficult realities a parent is ever faced with, proof they have not protected their child from harm. I felt responsible for all the awfulness that was happening around me. Was the whole world really full of terrible men just waiting to hurt little girls before they could even understand they were being hurt? If only I had convinced Sadie's mother not to let her take lessons with the Russian coach. Would this never have happened? Would it be better if I didn't exist altogether? Was I somehow drawing the darkness towards people? Like a magnet for bad experiences? These questions kept me up in the shower until my fingers and toes were prunes.

I spent the rest of the evening trying to do homework in front of MSN messenger. I pretended to go to bed at around ten. I lay there staring at the ceiling until I could hear my parents snoring from across the hall. I restarted my computer and logged back into MSN. There was no one to talk to. The few contacts I had evidently didn't have existential questions keeping them up at night.

A need not be alone led to me to Omegle. A chat website I knew I wasn't entirely allowed to be on. I began clicking through Omegle chats, filtering through the trolls and paedophiles asking me how old I was, did I like Justin Bieber and could I turn on my WebCam? It took ten minutes before the sense of danger and curiosity faded and the hopelessness returned. I can vividly remember telling myself if the next person I'm connected to isn't a goddamn decent human being, I'm going to kill myself.

5

911

The next person Omegle connected me to was Mark.

A twenty-one-year-old guy living somewhere in the US. We talked for nearly two hours. I trusted him enough to turn on my WebCam, to admit my real age, my real name. As I sat in front of him in my pyjamas and he asked what I was doing up so late the whole horrible story of my day came pouring out of me.

He listened carefully, then said it sounded like I'd done the best I could in a bad situation. It was very comforting to have someone who just listened to me with an endless fountain of empathy. He dismissed my fears that I was a magnet for bad people and that I was somehow dangerous for the people around me with well reasoned arguments. I'd never felt so clearly seen by another person.

His friends were there in the background of this conversation. They were smoking weed and having never tried it before, he eventually decided to partake also.

About half an hour, after they started smoking his friends left to get snacks from a gas station. I had no experience with any kind of drug, other than maybe a few glasses of lightly alcoholic punch and although I was uncomfortable I felt as though it would be uncool of me to tell Mark to stop. So, I sat with him on Omegle as he smoked more and more weed and got progressively less and less coherent and then began to get unwell.

My Google search history from that night consisted of things like how much weed is too much? Weed allergic reaction? Is it possible to overdose on weed? Can too much weed kill you?

As I listened to my new friend's breathing getting shallower and shallower, panic made me more reactive than thoughtful. I called the Australian emergency services in the hope that they would somehow be able to patch me through to their American counterparts.

I hurried through a rushed explanation of the predicament I was in and the response that came through from the other end of the line was a slightly annoyed, 'I'm sorry but we can only help you with emergencies within Australia.'

I wanted to scream, 'So what, I'm just supposed to let him die then?'

I hung up the phone. At that point, part of me wanted to just close my computer. Completely wash my hands of the whole situation.

What even was the emergency services line for the USA? I racked my brains drawing a blank. I remembered sitting on the green carpet of my kindergarten classroom learning the number that you could dial in emergencies to get help from police, firemen or an ambulance. At the time, that knowledge had made me feel so grown-up and in control of the world. Now, I felt like there should be some non-denominal hotline you could if you were in an emergency and didn't know the number. Shouldn't there be a service who could just connect you through to other countries? Like what if you knew about something really bad that was going to happen outside of your legal jurisdiction, were you just supposed to sit on your hands because there was an ocean between you and the bad thing?

Then somewhere from the deep recesses of my brain, proof that American's domination of the film and television industry is in some ways useful, came the number: 911.

Now here's the fun thing about calling 911 from an Australian landline. If you just dial 911, it actually doesn't get you very far. In fact, it redirects you to an automatic voicemail that tells you to call triple zero in an emergency. To actually place a call that goes to the US from Australia you need to dial a +1. However, this is where it gets even more fun as my circa 2010 landline phone didn't have a plus button.

In that moment as I read from my computer screen about the +1, it felt like I was doomed to fail. That Mark's friends would come back and find him dead on the bathroom floor. That I would listen to him taking his final breaths via the spectacular sound quality of 2010 Omegle video chat, but that I wouldn't be invited to the funeral. It felt like this whole awful day where I had comforted two girls after they had been assaulted would end in me listening to someone die, where there was not a thing I could do to stop it. In that moment, I thought that if Mark dies, I don't want to live.

Then I scrolled down to the next part of the page and found the instructions for calling from a landline phone. Dial 0011 1 911. It felt like the longest dial tone in the history of the world and then I heard a completely calm voice on the other end of the line say, '911, what's your emergency?'

I rapidly began to spit out the facts as fast as I could.

'Hi, my name is April Matthews and I'm calling from Sydney, Australia. But please don't hang up because this isn't a prank call. I'm calling about a boy called Mark and he's in a lot of trouble. He and his friends were smoking weed and I think that he's had too much, because his breathing has gotten really shallow and he's lying on the bathroom floor and he can't move. And his friends have gone to the store, so I really need someone to go there and smash down his door and take him to hospital. Please. He can't die okay because him and me, we're the same, okay, we're both scared kids and I really need him to live,' I choked out the last word, tears now streaming from my eyes.

Things started happening fast after that. There was some degree of difficulty in locating Mark's address, since I didn't actually know what it was. But eventually I was listening to a paramedic team break down the door and take him to hospital. I stayed on the line during the entire ride to the hospital and then was told by the paramedics that they were pretty sure I had just saved his life. I was given the number of the hospital, so I could call back the next day. I was then instructed by the paramedics to go to bed.

The next morning I remember feeling so grateful for the simple fact that the sun had risen on a new day. The worst day imaginable was over.

Nothing was really fixed though. Evil Science Teacher kept teaching. So did the Russian coach. Sadie kept skating until she was fifteen, but gradually more robotically, her joy for the sport slowly drying up like a puddle.

Mark ended up making a complete recovery, although he never wanted to touch weed again. He'll make an appearance again much later in this story, but his entrance then would seem random and surprising without this origin story of how we first met.

6

Lindsay: Warrior Princess

In the week following that Thursday, I continued to face Evil Science Teacher each morning and afternoon in homeroom. My despair gave way to a quiet rage that bubbled below the surface of my existence. I desperately wanted to fix the problem once and for all. I wanted it to stop. I hated that it had been allowed to continue this long.

The conventional wisdom offered to children in this situation is that we should tell a trusted adult and allow them to handle it. In my case the problem with offering this advice, is that I'd already lost faith in the ability of adults to fix problems like this one. It had been a long time since I'd held the idealised view that grown ups were in control and could prevent bad things from happening. Age did not, in my opinion, confer some magical problem solving ability. Adults were just as scared, just as messed up, just as willing to run away from things as children. My view on this was unwavering, and bolstered by my recent attempt to convince Sadie's mother not to let her take lessons with the Russian coach, where my suspicions had been dismissed as a dramatic overreaction, only to be proved correct less than a year later.

This view was also undeniably shaped by my own experiences with sexual abuse, a once or twice a year occurance perpetrated by a close friend of my father's who had lived in another state but come to "visit" regularly for as long as I could remember.

The end of this abuse was not due to the intervention of any of the number of capable adults in my life but prompted by a book I read. The book was from a series called *The Royal Diaries,* stories of real historical figures like Marie Antoinette or Anastasia Romanova told through fictitious diary entries. The book was called *Nzingha: Warrior Queen of Matamba, Angola, Africa.* I remember looking at the cover in the book store. On it stands a young woman holding a bow across her chest, a quiver of arrows strapped to her back. I remember not feeling terribly enthusiastic about the prospect of reading it. But I had liked the other books in the series with the European princesses, so I asked for it anyway.

The book itself provided a sort of revelation for my young mind. As the story begins Nzingha is twelve-years-old who is preparing to go to war. At time I was ten and I thought twelve seemed a reasonable age to go to war. Twelve, to my mind then, was no longer a child. At twelve, you could no longer hide behind the legs of your parents. At twelve, you had to fix your problems yourself.

But my twelfth birthday was still almost two full years away and there was something happening to me, that had been happening for a long time that I now understood to be wrong. Perhaps, I thought, under special circumstances ten-year-olds could also go to war?

And it was that idea, the idea that children could go to war that propelled me to beg my parents to stay at the abuser's house when we visited family in Melbourne over the Christmas holidays. It was the conviction, that battle was required to end bad things, that made me open my mouth alone in the kitchen with my abuser's girlfriend and ask if they were ever going to have kids.

I remember her turning around in honeymoon haze of dopey love, looking past me into the distance and saying, 'Maybe someday.'

'Do you want them?' I pressed her for an answer.

'Yes…eventually. You know, when the time is right,' she was trying to seem nonchalant, as though it was a life decision on the same level as a hair cut, a road that could be left or taken without a material change in happiness.

I remember feeling cruel, I knew I was bursting a bubble of happiness, but I opened my mouth anyway. This was war, war sometimes involved being cruel. 'I don't think you should,' I told her firmly. I watched her face drop. 'At least not with him, find someone else,' I tried to soften it by offering another option.

'Why not?' she asked. 'Don't you like me?'

'No, I do like you. I just think you should find someone else.'

'That's not that easy, you know,' she replied sadly.

'You shouldn't have kids with him because he's a pedophile,' I told her, the words spilling out of me.

'Do you even know what that word means?' she asked, every word coated in horror.

It was the tone adults use when a child has dropped an entire plate of food on the floor but I had my answer ready, like the lines I'd learned for the school play. 'It's someone who does things they shouldn't do to children. Who touches them in places that are meant to be private,' I told her calmly.

'How do you know that he's doing that?'

'Because since I was four, whenever he comes to stay, he's been coming into my room after everyone is asleep. He touches me. He takes photographs. He says not to tell anyone because these are our special secret games. That's a pedophile. Isn't it?'

'Yes,' her eyes were full of furious tears.

'And he's going to do it again tonight. When he thinks you're asleep.'

'No! I won't sleep. I won't let him. I can tell your mum. It never needs to happen again.'

'Actually, I'd rather you pretend nothing is wrong. I'd rather you just put a big sharp knife under my pillow. And then you can come in and take a photograph of him. So we have evidence. Then in the morning you can tell my parents.'

After that I left her standing alone in the kitchen.

I remember feeling worried that she wouldn't do it. That someone would notice the knife was missing. In kindergarten, I'd gotten into trouble for taking the glitter pencils outside in my pocket at recess.

I was so relieved when I put my hand under my pillow that night and felt the cold ridges of the bread knife. I felt so calm about every part of the plan where I only had to rely on myself. It felt so easy to pull the knife from under the pillow. So easy, to press the knife against his neck and tell him we were done playing his 'games'.

I'm telling you this story because I think it reveals an important truth about my personality, that given the choice between running to an authority figure with a problem and attempting to fix the problem myself, I've always been more inclined to choose the latter. I guess I'm hoping that you'll understand, a least a little bit why I didn't just report Evil Science Teacher to another adult. Why I chose to deal with him using a method that was essentially very cruel to a lot of innocent bystanders, and that you won't judge me too harshly for that choice.

The next Monday I came home from school determined to sit at my desk until I found a solution. An action I could take that would stop Evil Science Teacher from hurting anyone else. I didn't feel as though I could report him, because it wasn't my story to tell. What was I supposed to say, this girl told me he did this to her, but I can't name her? I decided what I need to do was to start a rumour. A rumour so prolific it would follow him until he retired or ended up in jail, I didn't really care which. Then, I was struck by an idea that seemed equal parts cruel and effective.

I would make a Burn Book. A real life Burn Book, just like in the movie *Mean Girls*. I would write toxic lies and awful made-up rumours about students and teachers. I did consider just writing that Evil Science Teacher was a pedophile but I wanted an atomic bomb of rumours. I wanted juice. I wanted gossip. I didn't think that firing one bullet in his vague direction would have the same impact as multiple attacks. I would have preferred a sniper, but I couldn't afford to miss. I would have to hurt other people in the crossfire.

So, I set to work on my Burn Book choosing to write about both students and teachers. I decided on five students, including myself and three teachers. I thought if I was going to write awful things about other people the least I could do would be to write an equally awful entry about myself as well.

It was hard to pick people. I selected carefully and then struggled with the weight of what I was doing and changed the names only to change them back five minutes later. The whole thing made me feel sick to my stomach. I wondered about how anyone with a job at a gossip magazine could function with the reality of doing this on a daily basis.

At some point, I just decided I was done with writing about my classmates and moved on to the teachers. I included three teachers in my Burn Book. I wrote that one gave out the answers to exams, another sold drugs to students, and that the third, Evil Science Teacher was a pedophile. It was the only thing on the whole page that was true.

That night, I didn't sleep. I just waited in my bed. As the first cracks of dawn started to appear in the sky outside, I got up went to my computer and printed one copy of my Burn Book.

I took my copy to the local news agency and asked how much it was to photocopy a document.

'Black and white or colour,' they said.

'Black and white,' I decided.

'How many?'

'One hundred,' I said. That had to be enough.

It was a total of four dollars and twenty-five cents.

When I got to school, I begin to place my Burn Book Pages around. It was early enough that no one was there yet. I thought carefully about the distribution of each of the pieces of paper, at least for the first twenty five copies. After that, I just started throwing them on the floor. I was slightly panicked that I had taken too long and someone would arrive to see me with the remaining stack of copies.

When I was done, I went back to sit by the fish pond. I wasn't sure how to feel. Part of me was fighting the urge to run back through the school and collect every piece of paper. I didn't like the idea of hurting people. I saw it as a necessary evil though. I made myself sit by the pond until I was sure it was too late.

As I could hear the school start to come to life, I made my way to my locker. Heads turned in my direction as I walked past them. Their stares gave me the awful prickly feeling of being judged. None of the pieces of paper still on floor were there anymore but it was clear they had been read. I pretended not to notice that anything was wrong. I collected my books and then went to hide in the bathroom until the start of roll call.

My Burn Book created a significant uproar, that seemed to ripple out through the school like wildfire. It took a while for the teachers to mount a response. The morning classes proceeded almost as normal, par a greater degree of whispering and less focus. Then in the afternoon every student I'd named in the book was hauled into meetings with the principal. She met with us together and asked if we had any idea who was responsible.

The other girls shook their heads and stared at the floor. I thought about confessing then, but it felt too difficult with only the girls I'd written about and the principal in the room. Also, I wanted it to give it enough time to work, I couldn't admit most of it was made-up before it had the time to set. So instead, I held my tongue and did my best impression of horrified cluelessness.

When this meeting didn't produce the name of the person responsible, we were sent back to class.

The next day, the teachers cancelled a double period of English to hold a meeting with our entire year group.

The teacher nominated to speak to us began, 'We want to have a meeting with you all to talk about this,' he held up a copy of the Burn Book Page. 'But to be quite honest, we don't know how to deal with this. It's taken on a life of its own. Initially we thought this entire thing was nothing more than malicious lies, but a parent has reached out to us confirming the truth of one of the allegations made here, which are very serious and police have been called in to investigate all the claims made about staff. So we want to open it up to all of you now, if anyone wants to tell us something about this, please speak up now.'

There were a few minutes of total silence. No one wanted to talk about it. The teachers took turns trying to prod us into speaking, with various unconvincing integration tactics.

There was a lot of, 'We really are going to sit here until someone speaks,' which was followed by silence.

'However long it takes,' more silence.

'We don't want to eat into your lunch break and cancel more classes, but we absolutely will if we have to,' the silence continued.

The next teacher in the lineup tried anger 'Really! No one has anything they'd like to say?'

'I find that quite unbelievable.'

'I think it's cowardly to hide behind anonymity and not to put your own name on your work.'

'We clearly know it's someone in this year group.'

Then they turned to the tactic of calling on girls at random, which made almost everyone in the assembled group become very interested in the ground.

When it was the turn of Ms S, the teacher who I'd accused of being a drug dealer, she searched the crowd of students for a minute. Her eyes locked with mine. She looked directly at me and asked, 'April, anything you want to say?'

Every head snapped towards me. There was a moment where I said nothing. I hadn't really planned for the aftermath, hadn't made any decisions about it all. It had been hard enough to make the ugly sheet of paper in the first place. But if the claims about teachers were being investigated maybe that was enough. Maybe there was no need to let the clumsy interrogation of our year group continue.

So, I got to my feet.

'I don't think any of you know how hard it is to be a teenage girl right now. How scary it is. I don't think any of you remember. I don't want to speak for anyone else, but there are so many things that are just really awful or really scary or both. So yeah, I wrote it. I wrote the Burn Book thing and yeah, most of it, nearly all of it is completely made-up lies. But there's one thing in it I wrote about a teacher I know is true. That I've known is true since the first week I started here, three years ago and sometimes to get the truth out you have to hurt people in the process. So I'm sorry to the people who I've hurt by doing this. But I'm not sorry I did it. I had to do it. I'm so so sorry but it happened and then it kept happening and I couldn't let it keep going like this.'

There was a moment of almost complete silence after I finished speaking. Then the teachers began saying things again.

I remember thinking that it was quite possible I'd spend the entire rest of my education, being completely hated by every other student. That it was possible I would be expelled. How would I explain that to my parents?

Sorry mum and dad, but I can't go to school tomorrow because I've been expelled for publishing malicious slander about five students and two teachers because I couldn't stand to put another broken girl back together in a place that was meant to be "safe." But I didn't feel like I should report an assault that didn't happen to me. So making a Burn Book which was very mean and untrue apart from the bit that was most definitely very true felt like the best course of action.

I can't remember who suggested this, but it was decided somehow that the best use of the rest of the period was to lean into the *Mean Girls* motif and reenact the scene where they all do trust falls from a stage. It seemed equal parts healing and cringe, but enough people wanted to do it that the teachers agreed.

So, for about the next half hour, we all crowded around the first step of an outdoor amphitheatre, watched girls mount the step to confess things. Things they regretted, people they'd hurt, apologies they wanted to make. Each of my classmates gave a speech then turned around a fell backwards into the arms of a mob of friends and acquaintances. Everyone was caught, held up and passed through the crowd.

One girl went up and said that there was nothing she wanted to apologise for but it might be the only opportunity in her life to crowd surf, so that she felt she'd better take it.

I went last. I felt like I should be last because if no one wanted to catch me and my head smashed into the orange concrete tiles then at least everyone who wanted to go already had. My speech was word vomit. I spoke about how in the movie Lindsay Lohan's character Cady, never made one of these apologies. That she's waiting in line as Janice is speaking but she never gets to the do the trust fall thing herself. That if you watch the movie, she has a piece of paper pressed in her hand. I said I wondered what was on that piece of paper. If it was a good apology. That catching everyone else had made me wonder about how to give a good apology when you hurt another woman.

That it made me remember my first day of high school, where my mother had been pissed that another parent she knew was also sending her daughter here. That my mother had whispered that the other woman was an evil bitch to a friend standing next to her. That afterwards I had frog marched my mother off, and told her very severely that she should never say something like that about another woman. At first, she had tried to bluster off with a you can't possibly understand the situation you're just a kid and I had argued back at her until I'd seen the shame stinging in my mothers eyes. That as I had been about to walk away the friend standing next her had asked if there was anything I wanted to say to her about it, and that I had replied that there was a special place in hell for women who didn't support other women.

My verbal diarrhoea ended and I brought myself back to the point I was trying to make.

That I knew I'd hurt other girls, other women standing in front of me. That I had been trying to help fix another problem but that didn't lesson the hurt I'd caused. That sorry didn't begin to cover it. That it didn't absolve me of anything I'd done and that I was okay with going to hell for the hurt I'd caused.

I turned then and let myself fall.

And they caught me.

7

Gardening and Debt Repayment

After my apology speech, I was marched to the principal's office. I sat on the dark green couch where I had been the day before but this time I was here alone. Maybe ten minutes passed before she called me in.

I was expecting rage. I was expecting anger. I was expecting her to have some kind of fury but initially she just sat and looked at me over the top of her desk. She was wearing reading glasses with green frames. I sat there waiting.

When she finally spoke it was a simple question, 'Why?' she asked me.

'Do you remember the day we met? My interview before I started year seven?' I asked.

'Vaguely,' she replied. 'I interview every enrolling student...'

'And it was a long time ago,' I finished her sentence. 'At the end, you sent my parents out of the room and you asked me if there was anything I wanted to know.'

'Yes?' she said slowly.

'And I said that the school grounds seemed like a beautiful garden, and you said that you agreed. And then I asked you if there were any snakes in your garden and you said you didn't know what I meant and I told you.'

'I said I didn't think there were any snakes,' she answered.

'Yeah. Well, I found one.'

'And what do you think I should do about it?' she asked thoughtfully.

'That's your choice. This is your garden.'

'And what do you think I should do about you?'

'I think there should be consequences. For what I've done. It's hurt people.'

She nodded her head. 'Wait outside for a bit. I need to think about this.'

The decision she made was that I was suspended from school for a week. I was given a letter to take home to my parents explaining the suspension. They were meant to sign it. I was told to go home.

I was grabbing books from my locker when Ms S approached me.

'Can we have a chat?' she asked, her tone casual as though we were friends deciding to get coffee together. It wasn't really a question though, there was an underlying anger that told me I'd better not refuse her.

'Sure,' I stretched out the word, 'Here? Or…' the question hung in the air between us.

'I was thinking in my office,' she said. 'Which I still have, no thanks to you,' the barb was carefully aimed.

I followed her to her office.

'So,' she began, 'What did you get?'

'Suspended.'

'How long?' she asked.

'A week.'

'You should be expelled.'

'I know… I want to say I'm sorry.'

'Oh, oh you're sorry. That's great. The police searched my

office, my car, my house. But you're sorry! You could have cost me my career! Did you think about that?'

'I had to do it,' I said simply.

'Right, so you're suspended. What else?'

'I'm not sure. There's a letter for my parents to sign.'

'That's it?' she was incredulous.

'Yes.'

'Okay, we need to talk about what you're doing for me then.'

'Okay.'

'Because I think considering the damage you've done to my life, I really should get something out of this little stunt. Don't you think that's fair?'

'Sure,' I replied evenly. 'I'm not sure there's anything I can give you though… Do you want money?'

'Do you have any money?' she asked with a laugh.

'I mean I have some. How much do you want? We could set up a payment plan. You could charge me interest.'

'Hmm. Tempting. I'm afraid it's also very illegal. Though perhaps not quite as illegal as selling drugs to students.'

'So did you have something else in mind? Or did you want me to write you an IOU?' I asked.

'Oh there's something. I've been coaching a quiz team at Newington Boys to make extra cash on the side. Preparing them for a science competition. It looks better if they have a girl on their team. Optics wise,' she paused for a moment.

'Makes sense,' I supplied in the empty silence.

'Also it would be good for them to meet a girl,' she added. 'The competition is Friday Night at their school. Can you be there?'

'I'm not sure. I'll probably be grounded once I show this to my parents,' I held up the letter.

'You'll figure it out,' she replied cooly.

'Okay.' I agreed. 'Is that all?'

'Depends.'

'On?'

'How well you do.'

'Right,' was all I could say in response.

When I got home I showed the letter to my dad, asked him to sign it and not tell my mother. Of the two of them, she was the one I was more scared of. He read it and asked if I wanted to explain what had happened. I said I did not. He gave me a lecture about taking responsibility for my actions and told me I was banned from my computer for the week but agreed to sign it without telling her.

So, began my week of suspension. I got up every morning at the same time and put on my school uniform. I was dropped at the bus stop at exactly the same time as usual. I waited there until my mother's car disappeared into the distance and then I walked back home, where my dad let me back in.

There was a booklet of required work sent to me to complete over the week. Though without distractions and banned from my computer it didn't take long for me to finish all the assigned work.

On the second day of this routine, I convinced my dad that my being at home with nothing to do would only annoy him and stop him from working. So, I was permitted to catch a bus to the ice rink, and spend part of my day practicing during the public session. After which I would put my school uniform back on and catch the bus back to the last stop on the school route, where I would stand in my usual spot and wait for my mother to collect me.

At midday on the Friday, the third day of my suspension and the day I was supposed to be going to Newington to participate in the quiz competition, I got an email from Ms S asking if I would be allowed to attend. I hadn't even attempted to broach the subject with my Dad. I sent back an email saying as much. I got a response within a minute asking why. I replied explaining I had been waiting for the best time to ask because although my Dad had been willing to keep the suspension secret from my mother, my being at home for the past three days when he was used to having the house to himself had been a significant inconvenience.

He was eating a meat pie with pea and ham soup when I walked into the living room to plead my case. After I stumbled through an explanation of the situation, I got the reply of 'I need to think about it,' followed by 'You're meant to be grounded,' which I then went back to the family computer and relayed to Ms S.

Again the reply came within a minute, 'Is there anything I can do?'

In the end, Ms S called my Dad to ask personally if I could attend and after ten minutes on the phone to her, he relented and agreed to take me to Newington.

The competition itself is a blur to me. I remember being introduced to my team mates in the five minutes before and sitting behind a table waiting for the event to start under very bright lights.

I don't remember the content of a single question. I don't remember the scores.

I know we won. That afterwards Ms S whispered in my ear that we were even and Dad drove me to an evening synchronised skating practice I'd already missed half of.

I don't think I ever comprehended at the time that the gossip about my actions spread as much as it did. I expected it to go everywhere in the school and I was right. It did. It was a lasting legacy and I expected it to stay with me until I graduated. What I didn't expect was to attend at a university with fifty thousand students and have people who I'd never met, who'd never been to my school, who could only know about me from gossip greet me as Lindsay or Regina. It was those interactions that made me realise how far and wide the rumours about me had truly travelled.

8

An Ugly Summer

In the summer that followed that year, I looked for a source of relief to my teenage insecurities. I felt lonely, ugly and empty. These feelings were overwhelming and hard to escape. I turned to something I could control, what went into my mouth. It was something I could be sure to do right. To do perfectly. All I had to do was follow every food rule I made for myself or found on the dieting Tumblr blogs. In a world that felt turbulent and unruly, the rules felt like an anchor holding me to the ground.

Every morning began with a weigh in, that was recorded diligently in my food book. My first meal was an UP & GO liquid breakfast and a big glass of water. I did not permit myself to eat anything solid until lunchtime. Lunch always contained one vegetable serving, and one protein serving, so half a chopped carrot and five pieces of chopped sausage.

Between lunch and dinner was afternoon exercise where I pushed my body as far as my limited energy levels would allow.

Dinner was a meal I both loved and dreaded to equal degrees. It was the only meal we ate as a family and thus the only meal where I was required to have a human sized portion. The only meal that ever involved any traditional carbohydrates like bread, pasta or rice.

Every calorie was recorded and scrutinised. Every night I went to bed exhausted and cold and every morning I got up and repeated the same steps as the day before.

Of course, my disordered eating habits resulted in a substantial weight loss and, of course, everyone noticed. The compliments came in thick and fast, and I saw them as pats of affirmation. Clearly, I was doing the right thing.

When I felt hungry, it was the right thing. When I could feel the sides of my stomach contracting as though the organ was eating away at itself, it was the right thing. When random places in my legs or arms would twitch throughout the day, it was the right thing.

When my hair began to fall out, it was a sign I was finally getting skinny. When my period stopped, maybe I was thin enough. When I started getting chest pains, maybe, just maybe I'd lost enough weight.

But maybe just another two kilos, after all, it would be nice to land on an even number.

The truth was I was starving. Deep down, I knew it too. I was faintly aware, in the back of my mind that my body was in a very ugly place. A battleground where different systems fought for resources. Like a person with unmanageable debts choosing which bills to pay, my body was choosing which systems to keep running. Eventually, there would be nothing left for it to run on.

My mother saw that too. At first, she fought me in covert ways, she started buying packets of TimTams, chips and punnets of ice cream. She cooked more food than our family of three would ever eat for dinner, so that the fridge was filled to the brim with leftovers. She made me snacks in the afternoons and delivered them to my room. But being surrounded by food only made me more devoted to the rules my eating disorder had created.

Eventually, as I came deliciously close to my ultimate goal weight, the weight at which I had convinced myself I would only need to maintain, no longer try to lose, she confronted me.

I was dressed for a friend's birthday party, wearing a red silk pyjama set designed to fit a ten-year-old and red lipstick. I felt pretty and pleased with myself that the pyjamas were looser then when I tried them on, just a few days ago. I was walking through the kitchen, there was a bowl with chicken schnitzel, broccoli and rice sitting on the counter.

'I made you dinner, April.'

'Oh, that's okay Mum, there'll be lots of food at the party. And cake,' I added as an afterthought.

'April, you will eat this, or you won't be going to the party.' Her voice was grim.

'But Mum if I eat now, I won't have any room for the party food,' I tried to protest.

'I don't care. Eat this or you're not going.'

I took the bowl off the counter and stomped dramatically to the dining room table. She followed me and came and sat down across from me.

'Do you know why I'm doing this?'

I looked down at my plate, not answering her.

'Because you're too thin, April and if you lose any more weight, you won't be skating any more.'

I looked up incredulously. Skating was the centre of my teenage existence. I had almost entirely stopped hanging out with girls from school in favour of my friendships with the skating girls. It was the thing that brought me the most joy in the world. It was everything to me.

'That's blackmail.' I said angrily.

'Yes,' she said. 'Whatever it takes.'

I picked up my fork and began to eat.

9

Heaven or Russia

As I fell into destructive eating habits, the Russian Coach began struggling with an even more lethal affliction, a combination of drugs and alcohol. I believe at first that he turned to them as a way to combat the rot, a way to suppress his thoughts and urges. Because I knew what he was struggling against, I regarded his growing addiction differently to everyone around me. When he showed up drunk to coach, I felt comforted by it, instead of disgusted or worried. I preferred the version of him that was skeletal and unhealthy. The version that was suffering. Maybe that was cruel of me.

Gradually, as time went by, his addiction became a natural part of the social fabric that surrounded me at the rink. The same as I noticed when another coach had a new haircut, I noticed when Russian Coach had brushed his teeth with Vodka. There were times when he was sent home to sleep it off. Times when I'm sure his colleagues tried to intervene. To halt the path of destruction he was forging. It made people worried or sad or scared. Mostly, I remained indifferent to whatever gossip about Russian Coach reached my ears. I told myself that I did not care what happened to him. He did not deserve my compassion.

That changed on a Saturday morning late in the September of 2012. It was around 7am, I was standing by the side of the barrier. Russian Coach had arrived at the rink that morning in no condition to coach anyone, and seeing this, one of the other coaches had told him to go home. He hadn't made it there though. In fact, he'd barely made it outside the glass doors that separated the inside of the rink and the parking lot. When you skated down the bottom end of the rink, you could see him sprawled on the pavement, just outside the exit door.

It was pity I think that made me jump off the ice, pick up my guards and my mobile phone and go outside.

When I got outside the exit door I walked past him, putting a few metres between us. I stayed standing and for a moment I just looked down at him. The heroin had eaten away at his muscles. His eyes were sunken. He didn't even look capable of getting off the ground.

'Are you dying?' I asked.

'I don't know.'

'Do you want me to call an ambulance?'

'I don't know.'

I sat down on the pavement.

'Why did you come out?' he croaked.

'Because I think you're dying. What did you take?'

He listed the drug and the amount.

'Is that enough to kill you?' I asked.

'Maybe,' he said slowly. 'What's it like?'

'Death?'

He nodded.

'I don't know,' I said. 'I've never died.'

'What do you think it's like?'

The only book I'd ever read where they'd really talked about death was *Harry Potter* so I decided to borrow from it.

'Some people say it's as easy as falling asleep.'

'Do…do you think we go anywhere?'

'Like Heaven, you mean? Or hell?' I paused. 'Maybe.'

'What do you think it's like?'

I tried to think of an answer he would like. 'Maybe it's like Russia,' I said. I could see by the way his face darkened that this wasn't a comforting answer. I tried again. 'I don't mean the bad parts. Maybe Heaven is just a long sheet of ice, that you can just glide forever on, like a never-ending lake, and you just feel the wind in your hair and keep gliding. Would you like that?'

He smiled at me.

'Close your eyes and try to go there now. I'll call an ambulance.' I dialled triple zero on my phone.

An automated voice asked me if I needed police, ambulance or fire services. I said 'Ambulance,' in my clearest voice and waited as I was connected with an operator.

I began with the address, 'Canterbury Olympic Ice Rink, Phillips Avenue, Canterbury, please send an ambulance now.'

'Okay, what is the emergency you need an ambulance for?' asked the operator.

'One of the coaches, he isn't feeling well. We're in the parking lot and he can't walk.'

'Why can't he walk honey?' the operator had picked up on the youth in my voice.

'Because he's taken a lot of heroin.'

'How much?'

'I don't know. Enough. Are you sending the ambulance?'

'Yes, I am. They are on their way to you. Do you want me to send the police as well?'

'No.'

'Are you sure about that? How old are you? Is there anyone else there?'

I ignored the question about my age. 'I only asked for the

ambulance. So I only need the ambulance,' I said firmly.

'Sweetheart, I'm only asking because that drug is illegal, and you sound quite young to be dealing with this. Are you sure you don't need me to dispatch a police car?'

'I know heroin is illegal. If he lives the police can talk to him then.'

'Okay,' she relented. 'Stay on the line with me. The ambulance is a few minutes away.'

I waited with my barely conscious patient for another two minutes until the ambulance pulled up. The paramedics jumped out immediately ready for action. Within another three minutes Russian Coach was completely loaded into the ambulance.

The paramedics turned back to me, 'You riding with us?' one of them asked me.

I considered it for a second and then shook my head. 'Do your best,' I said quietly as they closed the doors.

Russian coach died in the ambulance on the way to the hospital. I was the last person he ever spoke to.

10

The Chapter Where Nothing Much Happens

There is a gap in this story. This chapter is that gap. A void that contains nothing much of anything.

This unfortunate gap is the result of the fact that in real people's lives, the most interesting events rarely happen in a perfect sequential order. At times, day or months or years of simple ordinariness go by without anything truly notable happening.

This was the case for me. The three years between fifteen and eighteen passed without a significant event.

There were events significant to me. But nothing so special or impressive that it warrants an inclusion here.

Or maybe that's a lie I'm telling myself. Maybe there are some things that should in this chapter. But I can't make them fit. Or I don't know how to write about them.

So there's a gap. An empty space, I don't know how to fill.

It would be simple to execute this time jump in a film. There would be a soft fade from the last scene to black and a graphic that read 'Three years later' would slide into the bottom left hand corner of the screen as the next scene begins.

Or there would be sequential shots of calendar pages turning. Or maybe the changing of some kind of object to indicate the time passing, a stack of diaries piling up on a bookshelf, or a wardrobe that gradually fills with different kinds of clothes. Perhaps from here on the actress would wear her hair differently and the make-up artist would use a larger amount of eyeliner. Or maybe a different actress would take over the role, older, but similar enough to her younger counterpart that you could be sure it was the same character.

In fiction, this time jump isn't as pretty. The absence of things to put on a page is just a blank page.

I suppose you'll just have to take my word for it that between the last chapter and those that follow, three years did go by. And things happened. But I can't talk about them.

11

Perfect

We've been together a while now. Ten chapters. So I guess it's fair to say that by this point you have a pretty good idea of who I am.

In this chapter, I want to talk about something you may have noticed. A defining character trait if you will. I'm a perfectionist. I was a perfectionist.

If someone had asked me at eighteen to boil every aspect of my personality down to one word, that would be it. Perfectionist. Perfect. It's a subjective word. What is perfect anyway? I wanted to be perfect, but what does that mean really?

I'm realising now it's all very well to say this to you. To title a chapter 'Perfect' and call myself a perfectionist. But can I prove it? What are the nitty gritty details that will actually convince you this is true?

I've already told you about the summer (and six months following) that I didn't eat very much. Perfectionist and anorexia nervosa are extremely compatible bedfellows. That's common knowledge. But is writing about my eating disorder enough to truely paint the picture? Perfectionism is usually about controlling more than just one aspect of your life.

I haven't mentioned how even after I started to eat again, I still started every day by stepping on a rusty white scale and recording my weight in the front page of my diary. Or how I felt like two and half hours of exercise was a bare minimum requirement of every day, no matter how sore or injured I happened to be.

I haven't talked about my complicated relationship with all forms of feedback. How I struggled to take compliments. Or how grades either filled me with intense self-loathing or a rush of elation, quickly followed by a panic that I would not be able to live up to this new standard I had now set for myself. That I found even being above average at something distressing and considered anything below that to be a form of personal torture.

The truth is there's lots of evidence there. Lots of things I could submit as proof of my perfectionistic nature, but somehow they don't feel convincing enough.

Describing my perfectionism is like trying to draw a portrait with a fidgety subject, no matter how many times I begin again on a fresh sheet of paper, I can't capture her features. She is elusive. Without fail after I sketch the outline, she will get up and come to look at the canvas.

'That doesn't look anything like me,' she will say indignantly.

'It's not finished,' I try to explain.

'Hmmm. Maybe you should stick to bowls of fruit?'

As I try to write about her, she stares over my shoulder, she points to the screen and whispers, 'You know the first rule of fight club?'

'Of course I do, I tell her. It's—.'

'A good rule,' she finishes for me.

She thinks that if I point her out to you, if I try to draw a portrait of her, I will inevitably fail to capture her likeness. That she won't seem perfect enough. That the very essence of being, her whole purpose in life will be invalidated. She will lose the thing she values most — the illusion that she doesn't exist.

I still want to talk about her though. I think it's important that you understand what my life was. Its contents. Before they are thrown out of a plane without a parachute. Before everything goes up in flames. Basically before it all goes to shit.

You will see the perfectionist has her claws in deep. She is the central tenet of my belief system. The part of me that makes the most decisions, that comes up with the solutions to problems, governs most of my daily life. She demands a rigid, preplanned schedule. It's planned so throughly and recorded so carefully that I have a very clear picture of exactly what was happening on any given day in my life.

For example, here is everything I did on Monday the 4th of August 2014:

4.30am — Open my eyes to turn off the alarm that's labelled as Rise and Shine with a snowflake emoji next to it. My first thought is an assessment of the level of soreness in my legs, and on particularly bad days my core and arms also. This assessment lasts as long as it takes to walk across the room to the light switch and back around the edge of the bed. I don't think about going back to sleep, I'm already on an internal countdown timer to my first event of the day. I automatically reach for the clothes that are laid out the night before over the heater beside my bed. I don't really use the heater apart from as a storage space for tomorrow's outfit. Not exactly rushing but not dawdling either I get dressed. Sports bra, tank top, underwear, stocking socks, tights, sneakers. Two jackets.

4.36am — I make my way back across the room to the adjoining bathroom, and stand in front of the mirror attempting unsuccessfully to wash the purplish circles under my eyes off my face. Hair goes up into a bun.

4.41am — I'm upstairs now, making breakfast. Two table spoons of yogurt and half a cup of muesli into a bowl. I ration myself to one 600ml tub of yogurt per week. Sometimes at the start of the week, I'll allow myself to pour the yogurt rather than spoon it but that usually means eating dry, practically dry museli by Saturday. I'm still hungry after I finish the bowl but I move on to the next task anyway. I double check the three bags I've packed contain all the items required for the next sixteen hours of my life.

4.47am — Back into the bathroom, brushing my teeth.

4.48am — Floss. Yes, I said it floss. I was that one per cent person who actually flossed. Morning and night.

4.50am — Start car, turn on the radio, always hoping for the next ten minutes to be music and not ads.

4.59am — Pull into Ice Rink parking lot. I'm usually the first car. It will take anywhere from two to ten minutes for the person opening that day to arrive. Usually, while I wait I unload my bags from the car and move them to the entrance where I stretch out my legs on the fence railing.

5.05am — Inside now, fifteen minutes of warming up off the ice.

5.21am — Put on skates.

5.30am — One lap of stroking, peanut, Russian stroking, slaloms: both feet, forwards and backwards, circles of crossovers two minutes each direction forwards and backwards, outside edges, inside edges, forward outside and inside three turns alternating feet, double three pattern, inside three choctaw pattern, bracket patterns, counter patterns, twizzle and loop pattern, lap of bunny-hops, three jump x 3, three three jump in a row, three jump loop x 3, sal x 3, toe x3, loop x 3, loop-loop, flip x 3, flip-loop, lutz prep, lutz x 3, lutz toe, lutz loop, backspin exercises, three jump backspin x 3, axel attempts from standstill x 3, axel attempts moving x 10, sal backspin, double sal attempts x 3, double toe preps, double toe attempts x 3, double loop preps, double loop attempts x 3. Two foot spin, cross foot spin, change upright, plain sit, sit change sit, bullet, broken leg, tuck, plain camel, back camel, camel change camel, camel sit, camel sit back spin, back camel back sit attempt, layback attempts, one lap of stroking.

7.00am — Get off the ice, skates off, dry the blades, change clothes, wash face, sunscreen, mascara.

7.32am — Walk to the train station.

7.44am — Board train to Central.

8.03am — Eddy Avenue exit, walk over to stand in bus queue.

8.08am — Board bus to Uni.

8.39am — Drink Up and Go in tute classroom before first class.

9.00am — First class begins. It's Society, Politics and the Media.

10.12am — Study in law library.

12pm — Microeconomics lecture

1pm — Marketing tute

2.17pm — Guzzle green tea and mango smoothie, walking back to law library

4pm — Business statistics lecture

5.55pm — Join line for bus back to Central

6.55pm — Back at rink, doing core exercises for about 45 minutes

7.40pm — Drive home, inhale dinner, repack bags, lay out clothes, shower, start micro reading, brush teeth and floss

8.40pm — In bed

It might not sound like the kind of life that would make someone happy. It was all rigidly scheduled two weeks in advance in colour coded blocks on my iPhone calendar.

Everyday was almost identical to same day the previous week. On weekends I worked as skating birthday party host, money that went towards skating lessons, travel expenses and smoothies. I was rarely awake after 9pm. I didn't really make time to hang out with friends. I didn't make use of the fact I could now drink alcohol, didn't go to parties, nightclubs, or bars. My life existed in three locations: the basement of my parents' house, the ice rink and the university where I was studying a double degree of commerce and media. Everyone I interacted with was either working, studying or living with me.

At times it was gruelling. I relied on the routine of my habits to keep the wheels turning. That, and the knowledge that I chosen this life for myself. There was no prodding parental figure in my life. No puppet master other than my self inflicted quest for perfection.

There wasn't really an end game, or a destination. I wasn't delaying my happiness to some day in the future, but all the joy in my life was derived from ticking the same boxes day after day. It's difficult not to look back on this relationship of task and fulfilment and miss the simplicity of it, want to somehow recapture it, dream about boarding a time machine and just go back to living as that version of myself. Even if it would change nothing, even if I had to live through it all again, knowing nothing would change and it would bring me back to exactly this moment. I still believe if I had the option to go back I wouldn't hesitate.

Maybe it's how tightly I'm holding onto these memories that makes the comparison between past and present so acutely painful but there's a certain point where letting go no longer feels like an option. Every day that passes is another day that the longing binds itself to you, until it feels as much a part of you as the bones of your ribcage.

12

Lighthearted Joke

In general, I'd say I don't have the best track record with romantic relationships. By August of 2014, I'd managed to reach the ripe old age of eighteen with zero record of any kind. Worrying about being unlovable and therefore forever alone had taken up a lot of space in my head in my early teens.

But in the eighth month of that year, I felt I'd officially moved through all the stages of lack of relationship grief into this kind of nirvana where I was totally fine with my status of being permanently and unequivocally alone.

Now, the desperately self-conscious fourteen-year-old who had lied to friends about her first kiss felt like a foolish little girl bargaining against the cards fate had dealt her, that maybe she could speak an experience into existence. The five year long crush I'd had on Jake, a spin cycle of hope, paralysing fear, denial, anger and sadness had stopped. The machine of feelings had been unplugged from the wall. Even the seventeen-year-old I'd been in January, who'd admitted she was mostly looking forward to starting university because of the opportunity to meet boys now felt light years away.

Somehow without any real work on my part, I'd been able to let go of all of it. Somewhere during the semester break on a family holiday in Europe, I'd walked into a museum or cafe and walked out with a distinctly different perspective on my non-existent love life.

The world was big and wide, and life was both too long and too short to be unhappily alone. I could be fulfilled in other ways. Think of all the things I could achieve with all the time I would save simply being ambivalent to all the supposed benefits of love.

Again, I did nothing to deserve the lifting of this weight off my shoulders but sitting on a green chair at 4.05pm waiting for the second business statistics lecture of the semester to start I was totally convinced I just wasn't one of those people who were meant to find love and I was totally at peace with it.

I didn't have that X-factor quality other girls had that made guys want to date them. Cool. Fine. Add to my list of character traits.

April: brunette, hazel eyes, perfectionist, 5'6, morning person, high pain tolerance, totally undateable.

It was just who I was. There was no point putting any more effort into trying to change it.

Anyway I'm sure you can see where this is going. It's so predictable, I almost feel like I'm recounting the plot of the most generic teen rom-com of all time.

Enter stage right. Boy in Hoodie. Late for class. Searches room for a seat. Still the second week of a first year subject, very few seats left. As he sees this Boy in Hoodie swears under his breath. Seat next to me. Boy in Hoodie almost walks past my row. It's too close to the front thinks Boy in Hoodie. Half a step past my row. The back rows are too full. Stops. Turns.

'May I?'

'Of course.'

He takes a the seat next to me.

'Hi, I'm Eugene,' his tone is bright, almost overwhelmingly so.

'April.'

'Nice to meet you, April.'

'You too.'

A Pause. He didn't as I expected become interested in his notebook or the ceiling, but continued to look at me. The stare made me uncomfortable but I couldn't really put my finger on why. Maybe it felt too familiar, like he knew something I didn't.

'How was your break?' This was my polite question intended to fill the remaining minutes before the lecturer called us to attention.

'It was really long actually,' he dragged out the syllables of the really with a boisterous energy.

I smiled, 'You know that's not usually what people say right?'

'Yeah,' A wry, confident smile settled on his face. 'After my first year I decided I wasn't really feeling the whole studying thing, went to Canada to teach skiing.'

'Wow! That sounds wonderful,' I said, meaning it.

'Ha yeah, I mean it was mostly drinking and partying, which is fun if you're into that…' He paused as though he was trying to gauge how "into" that I was. Then clearly having made a judgement on the matter, decided to add, 'But it does get old after a while.'

'So, now you're back after your sabbatical in Canada?'

'Yeah. I didn't spend the whole time there though. I did other stuff too.'

'Oh, what kind of stuff?'

'Tried to start a business.'

'Oh, neat. What kind of business? Would I have heard of

it?'

'Ah no. It was a massive fail actually. I feel like I'm talking too much about myself. What about you?'

At this moment the lecturer called the room to attention and began telling us something about statistics that flew out of my head the minute after I'd taken the final exam.

I want you to know, for the record, that I didn't cast aside my vision of my life living alone, with maybe a dog. I didn't start picturing dates or walks along the beach at sunset or anything like that. At least not that afternoon. After that lecture, I said nice meeting you, walked to the bus stop, caught the bus then the train, climbed the stairs to the ice rink's mini gym, did forty minutes of pilates, and then drove home. I didn't think much of it.

Moments that change your life are like that. So mundane, you never blink twice as they're happening. Nothing about them says sit up and pay attention, I'm going to be important later. They're glossy, and microscopic but undoubtedly they are there.

On the Saturday of that week, a little after two in the afternoon, I was halfway through fitting rental skates onto the feet of fifteen seven-year-olds. This was part of my weekend job as an ice skating birthday party host.

On Saturdays, we had about half-an-hour between when the horde of parents and children were let in and when the kids got onto the ice for their lesson.

Within this half hour, you had to introduce the Party Parent to the Shift Manager, explain how the day was going to run, and help anywhere from eight to twenty kids put their skates on correctly.

For me, it was the most stressful part of the shift. You were trying to make a good impression on what was typically a slightly stressed out mother, who was, at that point was wondering what had possessed her to book an ice skating party in the first place. You were waiting for enough kids to arrive to make a chaotic trip to skate hire and then you were racing against an internal clock trying to fit every pair of skates fast enough to be ready to get on the ice and teach a lesson at 2.30. Usually there were four or five parties running at the same time.

If 2.30 rolled around and the other party hosts got their group of kids on the ice and you didn't, then in the eyes of the watching group of parents you either looked incompetent or neglectful. Neither of which was fun.

Here's the kicker about this frantic rush, seven-year-olds don't usually know their own shoe size. So, you have to get good a guessing shoe sizes based on how much the kid reaches over the metre high counter in skate hire.

So anyway, I'm halfway around my little circle of seven-year-olds who are perched on the wooden benches in varying stages of securing the plastic blue skates to their feet. It's all under control. I have plenty of time left on the instinctual clock I've developed during the last three years of working this job.

So, I'm fitting the child's skates, making sure that the plastic buckles are done up tight enough for ankle support but not so tight that the kid's in pain. It's like an autopilot, like how I now feel about driving a car. I'm talking to the kids, about how the skates feel, and if they've been skating before, and if they're excited or nervous about getting on the ice.

In my head, I'm making a list of which kids are confident, which are in a neutral semi-nervous state and which are petrified, so I know what kind of lesson I'm about to teach on the skittles to zoomies spectrum. As I talk to them, I'm trying to be honest about what skating is like, and whether or not they'll fall over but still keep them in a confident headspace.

Also I'm trying to learn their names because knowing their names makes the lesson a lot easier to manage.

But I wasn't really concentrating on any of that. It was moving through my head, the same way you watch television during the commercials.

The thing I was really concentrating on, was trying to remember what Hoodie Boy's name was. On the off chance, he happened to be among the substantially smaller fraction of people who showed up to lectures in week three and also sat next to me again.

Evan, no, that's not it. Edward? No, not the Twilight vampire either. What other guys names actually start with an E? I know it started with E. Eustace, no that's the Malfoyesque my father will hear about this character from *The Voyage of the Dawn Treader*. No one in Sydney would name their kid Eustace. At least, likely not in this century. Although Gwyneth Paltrow did call her daughter Apple. So maybe? No. It definitely wasn't Eustace.

E. E! E? Dammit. It's totally gone. I'm good with names usually. I remember everything else he said! Just not his name. E. E. EEEEE. This isn't working. He probably won't show up. He, seemed like the gets excellent marks with minimal effort type, anyway.

You shouldn't be worrying about this, April, if your going to worry about anything worry about how much HSC Maths you've forgotten since last year and how unpleasantly full of Maths that reading you have to do tonight looked. E. E. E.

'Okay munchkins! Time to get on the ice! You excited? Everyone's skates feel okay? Good! Let's go.'

It is now the Monday following. Monday the 18th of August 2014. The clock on the wall read 4.03pm.

I am in exactly the same seat as the last Monday. The seat is about five rows back from the front of the row in the

Chemical Sciences building at UNSW. I know this because although my undergraduate degree had nothing remotely to do with science, three of my thirty-two subjects in my degree were scheduled in this room.

In the semesters following that year, I felt like the room was haunting me. The pull, I felt when I was back in that room to that particular chair, the desire to sit and retrace old footsteps was positively ghost like.

However, on that particular Monday afternoon in August that moss green seat with it's violently-flipping fold out desk held no special powers over me.

At 4.03pm, I was rejoicing the fact that Boy in Hoodie had not appeared yet. See, I was scolding myself, he's not coming, all that rumination for absolutely no reason.

As though summoned by my thoughts, at 4.04pm, Boy in Hoodie pushed through the heavy door, and strutted up the aisle.

'Is this seat free?' he asked.

'Sure,' I answered.

There was an open seat next to me on the right, but Boy in Hoodie made the considerably greater effort to squash through past my seat and sit in the other empty seat on my left hand side. He dumped his bag on the ground, it was clear he was excited about something, from the way he almost bounced in his seat.

The next words out of his mouth were, 'Did you remember my name?'

My first thought was shit, I'm about to look like such an inconsiderate jerk. Should I give that awkward spiel about how I'm normally really good with names? That actually despite all present evidence to the contrary, I actually have an excellent memory. Should I tell him I can remember an operation I had when I was three?

I was about to start this speech, when his name came back

to me. Completely out of nowhere the answer flew into my head, like all the essays I memorised but was always totally convinced I'd forgotten in the first ten to thirty seconds of the every exam.

'Eugene,' I told him.

His head dropped and he adopted a pouty expression. I knew it was mock disappointment but I played along anyway.

'Did you think I'd forget?' I asked him.

'I hoped you would, so I could tease you about it.' A broad smirk accompanies this admission.

'Tough luck,' I said as I mirrored his expression.

Let's take a moment to check in with my imaginary "catching feelings" fair ground game. I'm imagining one of those Love-O-Metres that appear in American rom-coms. You know the kind I mean, you hit with a hammer and depending on how far the light shoots up you win a different sized fluffy animal.

I think at this point maybe I've given one my tickets to the person in charge of this game and picked up the hammer but I'm not really going to try with my one swing. It will be a minimum effort attempt. When it's over there will be no fluffy animal coming home with me.

When I pictured my future, I still saw myself retiring alone in a tiny apartment in Paris, with a dog. The apartment must allow dogs. Does that mean it has to be a small dog? Ugh, I would have preferred a big dog, like a Dalmatian. Can they live in apartments? Problem for future April to deal with.

I think I've got a pretty good read on Eugene though. Intelligent. Possibly a bit geekish. A private school boy. One of the expensive ones. One year of his tuition could probably have paid for three of mine. Ambitious and always felt like an outsider, probably because the popular kids were all white. He compensated for the relative otherness of his Japanese skin by acting like he didn't care what anyone thought about him. The bravado is a defence mechanism that works on two levels — an aura of cool nonchalance and a way to bond with the children of entitled elites who are entertained by the craziest person in the room.

Skip forward two Mondays. Attendance is looking slimmer again. The subject is hard, it's one of those ones where at least one person in your tutorial is usually repeating. No one feels like confronting hard things on a Monday afternoon. I can feel myself slipping too. Maths was a doable slog in year 12. This feels more sloggish and less doable.

Eugene walks in ten minutes late, there's a glass panel in the door and he makes a silly face at me. I smile and make one back. This is sweet I think, we have a greeting.

He sits down next to me, says hey in the whispered undertone you use when a lecturer is speaking.

Hey, I whisper back.

Ten minutes pass, I'm lost. I've stopped understanding the content that's being presented on the slides. I decide to reach for a life-line or at least someone else to drown with. I'm picturing Jack and Rose except in this version of *The Titanic* there's no raft in sight. So we will both just fall into a sea of statistical equations, but I'll have a friend to retake the course with and I won't have to lie in tutorials next year when they ask me why I'm a second year taking a first-year subject. Eugene can just cheerfully admit we both failed last year and we can high five sarcastically about blowing an extra grand and a half on our degrees. It will be perfect.

Anyway so I ask Eugene to explain what our lecturer means and he gives me a whispered explanation, I almost understand. I revise my projected future, I'll be drowning alone, and sarcastically high-fiving myself next year.

The lecturer calls a break not long after this, and Eugene

asks what I did on the weekend. I say work. He asks about my job. I tell him what it is. He looks more delighted by this than is reasonable.

'So you like kids?' he drawls.

It's an odd question. I mean yes. I do. In theory, they are nice interesting like characters. But I'm also very committed to my little apartment in Paris with my dog.

'Sometimes. Skating can be tricky. Ice is slippery. I get cried on a lot.'

He's even more delighted with this answer. I'm about to understand the line of questioning.

'So... If we have kids, you'll be the stay at home mum?'

He reads the 'my parents are one of five and one of four respectively and went to university under the Whitlam government, and how dare you think I would take the privilege of university, a right afforded to only 0.5 of my gender for granted to be your trophy wife!' forming on my face and horrified quickly redirects:

'Kidding, I mean you'll probably be the bread winner and I'll be the stay at home dad.'

I can see he never meant to hurt me, he is used to richer girls who do not feel guilty asking their parents to pay for university and as my anger subsides, I hear something else in his quick rush to role reversal. An insecurity common to children of great privilege, a fear of shadows, of never being seen for who they are but forever painted by the brush of a legacy.

The conversation moves on awkwardly, he knows he has hit a nerve.

In the film I sometimes play in my head to entertain myself the conversation ends differently:

EUGENE
Kidding, I mean you'll probably be the bread winner and I'll be the stay at home Dad.

APRIL
So are we compiling a list of names already?

EUGENE
Yes! I like Buttercup, Cauliflower and Raspberry. Thoughts?

APRIL
You want three?

EUGENE
You're killing my creative energy here. We can debate quantities later.

APRIL
Oh Sorry, my bad. I was merely wondering how much of my soul I'd be selling to a multinational to keep you and the kids in the lifestyle you're accustomed to.

EUGENE
Probably all of it. My lifestyles pretty lavish.

APRIL
Believe me, I've noticed.

EUGENE
(mock horror)
Really? What gave me away?

APRIL
Google.

EUGENE
Ah. So, am I going to get any feedback on my names?

APRIL
I'll discuss it with my mother and get back to you.

EUGENE
Yes. Have your people call my people.

You're probably due for your periodic check in with my imaginary "catching feelings" carnival game. The apartment in Paris was dissolving before my eyes. I was suddenly more interested in Japan than I had ever been before in my life. I was too shy to actually ask what BMX was, so I turned to my ever faithful companion when I developed a crush. Cyber stalking. I was very thorough, I combed through years worth of Facebook posts and what I could see of friends' feeds.

The playful messages started appearing on my phone screen. I mean they were usually after 8.40pm so I would take my phone off the charger and trudge bleary eyed halfway up the stairs so the wifi would connect to my phone well enough to send a reply. I never confessed my actual bedtime. I always said 9.30-10. I thought that sounded cooler.

I felt extremely insecure about my ability to hold his attention. My deepest romantic connection to date had been watching my high school crush date many very pretty girls. I checked for profile picture updates and relationship status changes daily, steeling myself the day that I knew was coming. The day the picture would change and the new girlfriend would be found.

The week after that he arrived ten minutes late. I was sitting the in same row again this time because I was hoping he'd show up. He made a goofy face as he walked through the door. I made an equally goofy face. He pushed past me to sit on on my left side. It felt comfortable, like being around someone you knew you could trust.

'How was your week?' He began the conversation, we still had a few minutes before the lecture was supposed to begin.

'Okay. Yours?'

'It was okay, I guess. It was my birthday on the weekend.'

'Oh neat, what did you do?' I asked with casual politeness.

'Just dinner with some friends. Pretty low-key.'

'That sounds cool,' my tone was encouraging. I wanted to more.

'Nah, it wasn't that great.'

'Oh, how come?'

A small smile fluttered across his lips.

'I didn't get a kiss from you.'

I smiled back.

'You didn't invite me to your party.'

'Would you have come? If I had a party would you come and kissed me?' He rushed it out all at once.

'Have the party and find out,' I said flirtatiously, on impulse, before I could stop myself.

'Ok,' he stands up 'I'm off, to plan my party. Make a Facebook event, wanna come help me?'

I hesitate, then follow him out of the lecture theatre.

'Wow, Hermione are you sure you want to miss a class? You might miss vital information.'

'I can catch up.'

'This is cool you know. Us going home like a real boyfriend and girlfriend.'

'If you were my boyfriend you'd have offered to carry my books by now.'

He laughs, and tries to take the bag from me, I side step him.

'I'm a strong independent woman actually. I can carry my own bag.'

'What is chivalry dead?'

'Yeah, pretty much,' I replied.

'What the fuck? When did it die?'

'Mhmm,' I said. 'Now, I'm having a moral dilemma. It might be considered cheating to tell you. If you know something is going to happen in advance and you want to stop it happening is that cheating? What are the ethics of cheating?'

For ten steps, he made a wonderful well reasoned argument that everyone in life should cheat on everything, as the world was fucked and fundamentally unfair. For two steps, I made my counter argument. There was a girl walking beside us and listening to our conversation. I asked her to chose a winner. She picked him. There were consequences too terrible to repeat that will not be written here. He regretted ever debating me in the first place. Chloe, the girl beside him, ran away screaming. No, she didn't, she really wanted to though.

I asked him if he still wanted to debate on whether chivalry should live or die? I told him it was on life support and whatever he said it might die anyway. He said even if it was a losing case, he still wanted to try. I told him chivalry had stage four metastatic cancer. That it was on life support. I told him if we debated, I wanted to cheat since he had already proved that cheating was the superior way to live life in every capacity. And that my first act of cheating was I wanted declare a moderator.

Fresh, from the unthinkable consequences, Chloe, the girl from earlier, tried several clever tactics be considered for the role, an impersonations of Hermonie from the first Harry Potter film jumping out of her seat to answer Professor's Snape's questions. The improvised line I'm not an owl from the fourth film. And then finally stopping after a blond boy she didn't know and asking to punch him in the face, she relunctanly conceded defeat and let me call his sister as moderator.

He pulled out his phone to dial her number at once. I snatched it out his hand, 'where is your sister right now?' I asked.

'I dunno.'

'Somewhere doing something important for your sister has

been a strong independent woman for much longer than I have,'

'I mean she's 25 and a doctor and not Beyoncé.'

'Slander on the Beehive! Disrespecting Royalty my my, the unthinkable has made us bold.'

'I didn't mean to.'

'There is always a price to debate me. I will bring you great and terrible pain of a kind you yet cannot imagine. I already have that.'

'So eager for more torture?'

'Anything for you.'

'Don't say that. I might be tempted to test it.'

'I like tests. Did you get good marks in school?'

'The best,' I thought for a second and then continued, 'And the worst. I like pretending to be bad at things.'

'Why?'

'So, I can learn from other people.'

Our negotiations brought us to a chess board, his sister arrived from a bad first date to keep score and time keep, as I was expected at my self-imposed training session so their was time for only one game.

He wanted to let me win. I could see he written all over his face. Hear it in the way he asked me whether I wanted to play as white or black?

Again, I feigned stupidity because I wanted a boy to talk to me. 'It has been a long time since I've played which do you think I should start as?'

'White,' his voice was sure, as though this was the certain answer.

'I will be black,' then I say flipping the board dramatically around.

We played our chess match. Me deliberately trying to lose and him deliberately trying to let me win.

In the end, his sister flipped the board, 'You are both

wasting my time,' she said angrily.

She was right, of course. We were wasting time. Or playing the long game, depending on which way you looked at it.

Walking towards the bus line it begins to rain, soft droplets at first and then more pellet rain falling around us. I pull the hood of my jacket over my hair. He pauses for a moment, before asking something I think he has been wanting to know for a while.

'How old are you, April?'

'Eighteen.'

'Have you ever been in love?'

'That's an awfully personal question.'

'Yes it is, but it's completely up to you whether or not you want to answer it.'

'No. At least I don't believe so.'

'Have you ever been in lust?'

'Yes, definitely.'

He smiles a smile as if he knows everything and nothing at the same time.

As we stand in the bus line, he slowly puts his arm around me. In that moment, I'm tempted to ask if he wants to audition to be my ice dancing partner, but instead I just lean into the hug. Or the half of the hug he is giving me.

I barely remember any of the bus ride to Central, only that it felt like meeting someone you were sure was right for you in every way you could imagine and perhaps a few you didn't see coming.

Arriving at Central, it was raining lightly.

It was almost a kiss. Almost, the beginning of something. For a moment it felt like magic, and then I looked down at my shoes and said that we'd better go through the gates.

On that train ride I felt elated, giddy with the hope of truely being seen by someone. Someone who wanted to know me, for the person I was, not the many masks I wore while pretending.

Sometimes I like to freeze frame back to that moment, live in that memory, as though it could be enough just to be frozen right there at that bus stop.

Then we walked through the barrier gates and the moment had passed and I was walking away from a moment I later realised had really mattered.

13

The Boy from Starbucks

After work on Thursday afternoons, I went into the city to sit in a Starbucks near Central and help my friend Emily with her homework. This sounds like a selfless thing to do but really it was an excuse to keep going over the study notes that I'd spent hours crafting over my last year of schooling, that I now could not bear to throw away.

I was always early for these unofficial tutoring sessions and Emily, for one reason or another, Emily arrived consistently ten to fifteen minutes later than whatever time we agreed upon. I usually had time to read or people watch from the window above the street.

One Thursday at the Starbucks as I was siting in my usual spot overlooking the street, not paying attention to a book I had open in front of me. The book was something I felt like I should read. A classic. It was written by someone with a long Russian name I definitely couldn't pronounce. I wasn't enjoying it. I was looking up at the sky, thinking something along the lines of could this be any more boring, when he walked by. As he passed he happened to glance up at the window and our eyes locked for a second before he continued walking.

The next Thursday, I am siting in exactly the same spot and he walks by again. This time when he glances up and sees me, he stops where he is in the street. His body language seems to say what the hell… I don't have anywhere else to be, so he turns around and begins retracing his steps.

I crane my neck to see where he is going and pressing my arms against the slightly sticky bench that smells strongly of cleaning fluid, I watch as he enters the downstairs of Starbucks. When he comes upstairs my first thought is that he is cute, in a tall gangly boyish way. He has light brown hair and the complexion of someone who spends a lot of time indoors. I'm almost expecting him to come up and speak to me but instead he sits down at the table next to my own and pulls out a book. It's another one of those Russian authors with a complicated name.

After a little while I give up on my own book, and watch him read. It's hard not to give him my attention because he is muttering under his breath. I can make out a few of the words.

'Monica… Monica.'

Who is Monica? His girlfriend? If he has a girlfriend why does he keep staring at me?

'Game time decision.'

Equally puzzling. Perhaps he plays soccer? Maybe his girlfriend Monica is meeting him later tonight at his soccer match.

'Mexican jumping beans.'

What is he on? Maybe that's the name of the restaurant he's taking Monica to after his soccer game.

At that point, Emily arrives and I move into tutor mode, helping her with a chemistry equation she's struggling to balance. Then explaining a physics problem. We switch between the two subjects several times over the next hour and a half. It's our usual routine only today I feel like I have an audience because it seems like Coffee shop boy is listening to me as well.

For the next few weeks, as autumn turns to winter, my Thursday afternoons continue as normal. I arrive, wait for Emily, help her out with whatever Maths/Science/English homework she happens to be struggling with that particular week and then leave. Coffee Shop Boy is always there, sometimes with his laptop typing away furiously at the keyboard, sometimes pretending to read a book, sometimes just watching.

Eventually, he gives up on the illusion of pretending to be interested in something else and just sits there listening to my tutoring session with Emily. I can tell by this point that he wants to talk to me. I can also tell that he isn't so fond of my companion by the way he's rolling his eyes or exhaling frustrated little sighs whenever she asks me a question.

This all comes crashing to a head when he stands up and practically screams across the coffee shop.

'STOP IT, Monica. Just stop. I can't stand to watch another second of you explaining the same thing over and over again. She's never going to get it. You're wasting your time. Please let's just get out of here and go and see a movie. Or do anything else really.'

Most of the coffee shop is now watching me, waiting for my reaction.

I get to my feet and say, 'Are you done?'

He looks at me blankly as though I have just thrown a cold bucket of water over his head. I repeat myself.

'No, that's a genuine question. I'm going to need an answer. So I'm asking you, are you done? Have you said everything you wanted to say? Gotten it all out of your system?'

He is still looking at me like I am speaking a foreign language, but this time he manages to nod his head.

'Well, to start with let me introduce myself. My name isn't Monica. It isn't even Molly. Although that's what's written on this cup.' I lift the Starbucks plastic cup to show him.

'My name is April and this is my friend Emily. So, I think we've just established something. You don't know me. You may think you know me. You've been coming here all these weeks watching me. But this is two hours out of my whole week. So, you don't know me. You don't know Emily either. You think that I'm wasting my time explaining the same thing over and over. But if you were actually listening you'd know that what I'm explaining is space time relativity. It's a theory of Einstein's actually. Heard of him? Yeah, so, suffice to say it's a pretty complicated theory. That doesn't always make sense to people on the first explanation. You also don't know anything about my friendship with Emily. You don't know that I've known her since I was eleven. You don't know for example, that she helped me through my Dad's cancer last year. Actually, my Dad never had cancer but my point is you wouldn't have known that, because you don't know me. And, the funny thing is, I would have gone to a movie with you if you'd just asked me like a normal person. But now that we're screaming at each other in Starbucks, I think that ship has sailed. Don't you?'

As I finish I look to Emily. 'Anything to add?' I ask her.

She shakes her head.

'Cool, wanna get out of here, then?'

'Yeah, definitely.'

As we leave, Coffee Shop Boy is still sitting frozen to his seat, in shock over what had transpired in the last five minutes.

He didn't stay frozen in his seat however. He went on to write about me for a creative writing class and that's how my Thursday afternoons became a piece of writing called *The Girl in the Coffee Shop*. This piece of (not really) fiction got adopted as a sample for a university course. In my final semester I took the course. It was incredibly funny to hear what other people thought about the mysterious Girl in the Coffee Shop, but really the story wasn't about me, just a version of me that the Boy from Starbucks had created in his head.

14

Pig or Cow

There's this saying that bad things happen in threes. I tried to look up the reason for this. The answers the internet provided me with were less than stellar. One article suggested we are conditioned to recognise things in patterns of three. It pointed out examples like three acts in a play, the Holy Trinity, how Goldilocks encounters three bears and that Neapolitan ice cream has three flavours. I'm not sure whether this is true or not but so far, I've told you the story of my encounters with two boys, Boy in Hoodie, and Boy from the Coffee Shop, however there was a third boy in my life at the same time as the other two.

It's time for the final act. Boy with the Money. To be clear here, I'm not saying that the first two didn't have money but I know unequivocally that they didn't have as much as Henry.

Henry. I've debated a lot about whether he needs to be in this story and I've come to the conclusion that he does, although part of me feels guilty for including him. In many ways, Henry coming into my life was the spark for the fire that changed everything. Burned everything that surrounded me past the point of recognition. Henry wasn't to blame for that exactly, but he was one part of why things changed.

I met Henry in a Marketing Fundamentals class at Uni. The first week he arrived late, slouched in and sat at the back of the class. As the tutor marked the roll, I remember the room bristling as she said his name, heads snapping in his direction. I understand why now, but I didn't at the time.

That week we were each assigned a group to work with on a semester long project. Henry and I were put in the same group.

In actuality, Henry and I spent very little time together, a few minutes before class one week, an email about the assignment the next. The only time we ever had a decent conversation was in a block of empty time between two end of semester exams, where we chatted casually about part-time jobs, holidays, and what we thought would turn up on the impending exam. Of course, none of this changed anything in Henry's life, but it drastically altered mine. Being seen even these very few times with Henry changed the way people saw me. It was like I'd adopted a new personality trait. I went from my usual description of 18-year-old uni student with brown hair and hazel eyes to:

'Have you met April, no remember *April* I told you about her yesterday, she's so lovely, well she's friends, well maybe a bit more than friends with... yes, mhmm, well I mean I wouldn't say Gold Digger, but like he really needs to buy her a new car, because that Totoya Corolla she drives is really bringing down the mean value of the parking lot.'

Of course no one said that to my face. It was whispered between the figure skating parents over coffee, past around the university campus through pointed glances until somehow spilled out and became a fact that followed me almost everywhere I went. It didn't seem to matter that there was absolutely zero truth to the rumour that I was involved with Henry, it still wormed it's way under my skin. It became a part of my identity.

It spread so far and wide, that it even began to effect my interactions with strangers. At one point, I was standing in the ice rink canteen on a Thursday, waiting to pay for my toasted cheese sandwich, when a man I'd never met approached me and asked if I could buy him a coffee.

For a moment, my mind flitted to the possibility he was hitting on me, but he was at least in his forties and there wasn't even the hint of flirting in his tone. I also wondered why me? Why did he think I wanted to buy him a coffee? I looked down at the five dollars that I was buying lunch with and said, 'Sorry, no.'

He didn't react the way I had expected. He was incredulous. 'Why not?' His voice carried over the entire room as though he was trying to make a scene.

'I only have this,' I lifted the five dollars to show him.

He stared at the note in my hand and I wondered whether he was slightly unhinged.

'Are you saying you can't afford to?' He was looking at me, as though I had just said that I regularly travelled to Pluto for my haircut.

'Yes,'

'What about the black American Express he gave you?'

At this point, a staff member came over with my sandwich.

'What's the problem here?' she asked the man, her tone clipped and impolite.

'She,' the guy indicated me, 'says that she can't afford to buy me a coffee.'

'So?' The staff member looked deeply unimpressed with the guy.

'So, do you know who this is?' He was still speaking as though I was part of the wallpaper rather than a person. 'Do you know who she's with?'

'Yes, that's April, she's been coming here since she was eleven. Works in the shop just over there, selling skates. What did you sell the last pair for? Two million? Three?'

'Two hundred dollars,' I replied, the ice of understanding had entered my veins.

The man looked furiously at both of us, and stalked off, muttering something probably very impolite about rich bitches.

This was a dramatic example, but Henry changed my life in more subtle ways as well. Gradually, without my even noticing, things started to shift. Over the next weeks and months, people who had never looked twice at me before began to ingratiate themselves, wanting to be my friend. They asked odd questions, seeking my opinion on all kinds of things; everything from music, to shampoo, to what I wanted to call my future children. It felt like they were taking notes, filing this information away for future use, although from my perspective it didn't seem remotely useful.

Moving through the world felt different as well. It felt like I was now under a closer level of scrutiny, occasionally I'd feel like I was being followed as though even my movements from home, to the rink to uni and back in the reverse order were now somehow interesting. There was also this look I'd get sometimes on the train as though the stranger sitting across from me desperately wanted to ask me something.

This changes left me feeling unsettled and self-conscious. If I'm honest, they made me anxious. I didn't know what to do about them or how to explain them to anyone I trusted. So I said nothing.

The thing about greed is that in some cases it comes from need. And while I cannot defend every action, I understood them, I understood them thinking it was a happy fairytale and I was a princess completely safe in my pumpkin and no harm would ever come to me. I understood the desire. I understood the moral rationalising that goes on when a person who feels helpless to change their financial situation is provided with a quick, easy and painless way to do so. I understood the guy in the canteen and his demand that I pay for his coffee.

I am by no means claiming to be sure of the complete picture. Why? Imagine you are playing a game of Cluedo. You have about half the information you think you need to make an educated guess about the murder. Anxious to get to the answer before anyone else, you go to fill in the secret ballot.

To your surprise you open the envelope to find an entirely new set of instructions you know are not only required to solve one murder but sixteen other crimes of varying severity that occurred in the seven months prior. You have now gone from five suspects to twenty two, and some characters may have committed multiple offences.

Flummoxed by this change in circumstances, you find yourself trying to puzzle out a solution. This is the mental gymnastics exercise I went though, trying to piece together everything that was being said behind my back, to come to turns with this new inherited identity of rich girl, despite working two minimum wage jobs, and ultimately not knowing who I could really trust. Of course, my account must be taken with a grain of salt. I do not claim to know everything, even now.

Up until this moment, you could easily mistake my story for the clichéd, girl meets boy, boy is classically unavailable, until ten minutes before the end credits when they both realise that they are perfect for each other and credits roll to some upbeat pop song. And you wouldn't be wrong. That's the story I felt I was telling. I thought I was living that story. And maybe I was. Until I wasn't.

15
Spiraling

On the day we were due to get our end of semester grades back my phone lit up with a message from Eugene. The flirtiness that had once felt attached to these messages had cooled to a more polite exchange of pleasantries. As though we had both silently acknowledged that because nothing had happened to push things further so far it was unlikely that it would. I felt more bummed by this than I wanted to admit to myself.

Eugene was asking about my marks. I wasn't particularly worried about failing anything apart from statistics where I thought the universe might just fail me purely out of spite. I logged in to my email to search for my results. I'd passed everything even statistics. I relayed this information to Eugene, feeling like I was only being asked because we were in the same course and he wanted a point of comparison for his mark. I tried to drag the conversation out further by asking about his holiday plans, but got the kind of polite responses you give to someone when you don't really want to talk to them that much.

After that he stopped messaging me almost entirely. My world felt colder in the wake of his absence. My friends were either weirdly clingy or completely unavailable. Blaise who I normally would have shared everything with was suddenly too busy, at least for me.

I got lonely. So I packed more into my schedule in order to avoid my loneliness. It made my mind busier but it did nothing to strip the feeling of emptiness. It was like being in crowded room, without knowing anyone. Everyone around you seems absorbed in their own conversations. You feel tempted to scream, I'M HERE TOO.

Instead, I turned my worry and loneliness inward.

This is when I began noticing that things felt off. My life became like playing Pictionary with twenty to thirty people. I knew they were speaking in a code. It was a code I half understood, but chose to ignore to make them feel more comfortable about me. It was as though they had some delicious secret about me.

I realise as I write that, that it probably sounds pretty paranoid. But the evidence of things changing was fleeting, a woman who turned to watch me take off my makeup on the train, conversations that would come to an immediate halt when I entered the room, that feeling where all the hair on the back of your neck stands up, a sick feeling of wrongness that you can't shake.

Mostly I tried to put it aside. That worked until it didn't.

As I worried more and slept less, the pieces of the jigsaw seemed to finally fit together. I realised that someone was collecting information about me and my suspicion fell on the one person in my life I knew had the means to do this. Henry.

Henry was the reason I had a neighbour who walked up and down a tiny stretch of pavement outside her house. I saw her every time I left the house, mornings, afternoons. She never acknowledged me, just marched along her tiny stretch of pavement, ten metres one way ten metres back. She was watching for me.

Henry had me followed. Henry had probably hacked my phone, my computer. He was obsessed with me. He was the reason everyone in my life had been acting so weird. The reason some of my friends had been holding me at arms length for months and others had been acting sweet while squeezing me for information like a lemon. Of course, Henry had been paying them for information about me.

I was so close to completely putting together the jigsaw. However, there was one thing I got very wrong.

It wasn't Henry.

Most of the above was actually happening but there was a different person behind it.

Trying to cope with this realisation that my life had been watched like some kind of Sims computer game was overwhelming. I did the one thing I thought would make me feel better, the thing I hoped would put everything else in perspective. I went for a run.

After two hours, I ended up on the side of a busy road. I could go no further. I had to choose.

I could go to a police station, a hospital or into the traffic.

16

000

I was still sitting on the curb of the busy road when I decided on the ambulance. I felt sick. I hadn't slept well in over a week. When people feel sick, hospital is the logical place to go.

I looked down at my phone. For some reason making the call using my own phone felt too hard. I didn't know what to say. I felt anxious even touching it. I turned it over in my hands. I sat it face down on the road between my feet. The cover had blue and green stripes. I stared at the colours.

Around me the road was busy, full of cars going places. I tried to work up the courage to dial 000. I thought about the only other time in my life that I'd had a reason to ring that number. When it had been about someone else, I hadn't hesitated. I'd just done it but maybe fourteen year old me was braver than this current version?

I'm not particularly sure how long I sat there. More and more cars continued to buzz pass. The sky changed from a pre-dawn blue to the deeper sky blue of morning. Eventually, I knew I would have to ask someone else to make the call for me.

The intersection of the road I was on had a run down

petrol station. I approached a guy who was filling up his motorbike.

'Can you call me an ambulance?' I asked in a voice that felt very far away from my own.

He looked disappointed somehow. 'No. I can't.' He'd placed the emphasis on the I in a weird way. I just stood there, waiting for him to clarify somehow. Say something like I'm in a terrible rush. Or sorry.

Then he said, 'I can take you somewhere to get medical care but it won't be a hospital.'

For the second time that day I felt caught at a crossroads. What was this place that offered medical care but wasn't a hospital? Was he hitting on me in the weirdest way imaginable? The exhausted part of my brain that was just done with making decisions, wanted very much to say yes. To give all responsibility over to someone else and not think anymore. Make a reckless bad decision. Just forget consequences existed. I asked one more question though.

'If I go with you, it's permanent isn't it? It won't hurt anymore but I also won't see my family or friends again?'

He looked at me for a long moment, then nodded.

'I don't want that.'

'Then go inside and ask the attendant to call you an ambulance.'

Even now, I don't know what to make of this interaction. What was the place he would have taken me to, had I gotten onto that motorbike? Would it just have been some dingy apartment with an Xbox and a strong smell of weed? Would I have been locked in his basement for the next nine years? Would he have chopped up my body into pieces and fed it to his goldfish in tiny chunks?

Then there are my less probable theories. Like maybe I was having a conversation with death, not just a random guy on a motorbike. Maybe that was why he said I wouldn't be able to come back?

I'm not sure why it matters to me but that is one of the parts of this story where I feel like things could have gone a very different way. And maybe then I'd be writing a book about what it's like to have your limbs chopped off and fed to a goldfish.

Anyway, I followed the instructions of the man on the motorbike. I went into the petrol station which was really more of a mechanic who also happened to sell petrol and asked the first person I saw if he could call me an ambulance.

He was a middle aged man with a belly that protruded out over the front of his jeans. He looked tired although he had kind eyes.

'Why?' he asked, 'Is someone hurt?'

Again very suddenly it all became too much. I dissolved into a hysterical mess, sobbing on the floor.

Through my crying I tried to explain what had happened, and the overwhelming strain of it to this stranger.

He got me a chair to sit on and water to drink which I mostly just held between my shaking hands as we waited for an ambulance to arrive.

I had never been in an ambulance before. I kept coming back to that. It felt important. The same way your first day of school or your first day of work feel significant. It was a first. My first ride in an ambulance.

Mostly it was how I expected it to be. It had all the features you would expect to find. It smelled of cleaning fluid and air freshener.

I had perched myself on an available seat rather than the large stretcher bed that was pushed against one wall of the van. The paramedics buzzed around me, readying the ambulance to leave. There were two of them, a young blonde and an older guy probably in his mid fifties. They moved with that efficient kind of precision you see from people who know how to do their job well.

As we pulled away from the petrol station, the paramedics began to ask me questions. At first, they were simple questions that even a five year old could answer. What's your name? April. Last name? Matthews. How old are you April? Eighteen. Can you tell me your address and your phone number? They were incredibly simple questions. But I struggled to answer them. The more I spoke the more a soul sucking kind of panic seemed to overwhelm me.

As the grip of panic seemed to tighten around my airway, I wheezed and coughed and spluttered out responses. Eventually, my breathing got bad enough that they had to produce a paper bag for me to breathe into.

Breathing into the bag I managed to swallow some of the panic and the tears on my face dried into my skin. As soon as I could talk again the paramedics resumed their questions. However, now they were not so easy to answer. Why are you so anxious? What are you afraid of?

I couldn't find the words for my life feels like it's sliding out of control in all directions and I feel really scared by everything but most especially by the idea that someone is stalking me because I'm a normal person and I don't think anyone should pay me this kind of attention.

So instead, I told them a mixed up, garbled version of all the events that had led me to the side of the road.

It was hard to articulate the story in the correct order and I kept making mistakes and then backtracking to try and make them understand me as though everything depended on getting them to understand what I'd been through. As though that would somehow fix everything.

Then suddenly, as if a lot of time and no time at all had passed, we were pulling into the hospital emergency department.

I wanted to give the blonde paramedic a hug, because I knew I would never see her again and I felt like she had saved my life. I knew that she technically wasn't supposed to give me a hug, but I asked for one anyway. It was a moment of simple comfort. She radiated this 'it will be okay' vibe, that I tried to hold onto as she walked with me through the sliding doors of the emergency department.

I was taken to to a blank room with a chair and a bed. There was nothing on the walls and the bed was only a mattress. A nurse hovered by the door. She introduced herself and I who was normally so good with names, forgot what she said almost immediately. I felt exhausted from trying to explain myself in the ambulance. I still felt like I was on the verge of panic. There was nothing to do but sit and wait for the first of many doctors I would see that day.

The process of admission felt not unlike a set of job interviews spaced thirty minutes to two hours apart, where the doctor interviewing me would ask questions that came from a list in their head and make notes on a clipboard.

I didn't really know what job I was applying for. I had told the paramedics I wanted a drug that would knock me out for three days solid. A magic sleeping pill, the kind that makes that deep won't move for twelve hours sleep. I wanted to catch up on the sleep I'd lost, then go back to my regular life.

Had I known the end result in advance, had I known everything that follows I probably would have answered their questions a little differently. But I was blissfully unaware of the reality of the situation.

The first set of questions were basic and general.

What brought you here today, April?

Again, like in the ambulance, I struggled to find an answer that was both honest and coherent. I don't even remember what I said really.

There were about ten follow up questions related to my general health and wellbeing. Then the verdict of I'm going to get someone else to come and check on you soon.

So I waited. The next interview was about my eating habits but towards the end the questions shifted to drug and alcohol use.

I don't do drugs. And I rarely drink. Again, the same verdict of I'm going to get someone else to come and see you.

After the third interview I gave up trying to relax.

In the fourth I was asked, how would you rate your stress levels?

High and growing by the minute was what I wanted to say but instead my answer was the noncommittal, they're moderately okay.

'Have you been more stressed or less stressed than usual in the past week?'

'More than usual.'

'In the past month?'

'More than usual.'

'In the past month was there ever a time you felt so anxious that nothing could calm you down?'

'Yes, today.' I paused. 'That's why I'm here.'

It felt awkward being past from doctor to doctor, interview to interview like this. Sometimes they would repeat questions, it never seemed like they'd spoken to the previous person. I was just a paged message on their endless list of people to see. Another to do to tick off. Not a person really, just a set of questions that had been answered and could be summarised in a few lines of notes. And I know this is how the system works. How it has always worked. But nothing about it felt helpful or problem solving. It nothing for my sense of dread and panic. I wasn't reassured or comforted. It was all clinical.

I suppose if you go to hospital with a broken leg, things are simpler. There are pain killers given out immediately because shit, you have a broken leg. When you have a broken brain, there's no immediate solution.

Not that they didn't do physical tests. There was a blood test and urine sample. Both were difficult, because I was dehydrated from running for two hours. Anytime I asked for water, the nurse watching over produced a half filled plastic cup. She got frustrated with me asking for water pretty quickly and I didn't want to be a nuisance so I swallowed my thirst and stopped requesting water.

The next interview featured questions like:

'How would you rate your mood out of ten?'

'Five, no four and half. '

And...

'Have you been feeling paranoid at all?'

'Not before this morning.'

'Are you hearing voices, April? Seeing anything out of the ordinary?'

Then there was another hour of waiting. Staring at the pale yellow walls of the room, watching different combinations of patients, visitors, nurses and doctors bustle past the doorway.

The last few questions came from an older doctor with greying salt and pepper hair and glasses.

At the end of his questions came a verdict.

'We would like to admit you as an involuntary patient, April.'

Diagnosis is about putting people into a box. There's very little nuance to it. It's either box 1 or box 2. There is no alternative. Being an involuntary patient, as I would soon learn, means transferring a lot of your rights to someone else. Deciding that you can run someone else's life better than they can, is a big call. Do no harm seemed to go out the window. The hippocratic oath becomes 'Do it my way'.

17

Hippocratic

The waiting room of the place they took me to was pleasant enough. Nice looking couches, a television playing the Australian Open, a filtered water cooler, polite receptionists, soothing music. It looked like a fancy dentist's office. All that was missing were the signs about tooth decay and flossing. I just sat on the couch in front of the tennis match and cried. I'd been crying most of the day and I was beginning to wonder if I would ever run out of tears, but they seemed to keep appearing almost out of nowhere.

Eventually, two nurses approached me, although they weren't wearing the usual dark navy scrubs, just clip-on ID cards attached to the belt loop of their pants. My parents were behind them, carrying a parcel of belongings from home, although they felt like hollow shadows of themselves, all their personality and charm stripped away.

The first nurse's voice was clipped and determined.

'Okay, we all ready to go?'

She reminded me of a primary school teacher, herding a little brigade of children on a field trip.

My mother began in the voice she used when I was five. 'Okay, honey, it's time to—'

I cut her off. I didn't want to fight with her but I couldn't help myself.

'Mum! I know that *this* is bad alright, but that's no reason to treat me like a five-year-old.'

My mother opened her mouth and then shut it again. She looked like she might cry. I knew I wouldn't be able to bear that.

Silently, I asked her to pull it together. Just until the car ride home.

The nurses ushered us onto the ward.

As soon as we walked through those doors, I immediately knew this wasn't what I had signed up for. It felt like a human fish-bowl, complete with brightly coloured plastic coral. Somehow the brightness was hiding rot underneath.

We walked down the hall past about ten doors. The nurses stopped in front of a door. This will be my room they told me. They explained that on the desk were forms I needed to sign. Some recorded a list of my belongings, some were about the privacy of my medical records and a final form lists my new set of rights while I was here.

They explained that only certain things are allowed on the ward at certain times. The items not allowed all the time were kept in a locker and you had from 10.30am-11.00am each day to access this locker.

The older nurse sorted my things into two piles. One I could keep in my room and the other would go in my locker. The locker list included my phone, my hair ties, floss, and mouthwash.

Then the nurses left. I was allowed time alone with my parents. Precious little time to explain everything that had led up to me being here.

I tried. I didn't want to talk about it. I wanted someone to hand me a neatly written letter that explained everything in just enough detail so that they would understand, but not enough to scare them. But that letter was not going to appear. Instead, all I could offer was my limited understanding of the truth.

My parents are smart, capable people, I told myself, they will understand. They did understand in a way. I watched their eyes go wide with horror. And then pain. But they didn't believe me. They didn't think I was lying either.

They thought I was mad. In many ways they still do.

It was late afternoon when my parents left. I set about exploring my new surroundings. There were two long corridors of rooms that stretched out on either side of the central part of the ward. Plopped in the middle of the two corridors was a high counter with a blank white board behind it. Opposite the counter was a carpeted area with a television and couches. There was also a dinning area and cafeteria set-up where food could be served. There were doors to fenced off bits of grass, surrounded by some ugly looking bushes.

The bedrooms were furnished with inbuilt wooden cabinets and shelves, beside a small wooden desk. The beds were the thing that made the room look medical, with their painted metal frames and wheels. Next to each bedroom was a bathroom with speckled yellow walls and identical flooring.

The most interesting thing to me was the other patients, who at first mostly kept their distance. They didn't exactly seem unfriendly, but no one went out of their way to speak to me either.

One thing that did seem odd to me was that quite a number of the patients were leaving that day. A rail-thin woman told me she was setting off on a cruise. She didn't exactly look in the best of health, but she seemed very excited to be leaving. She gave me a hug goodbye, despite the fact that we'd only just met.

The afternoon passed without incident. Dinner was served at 5.30, fish with a disgustingly thick sauce, that seemed to be made entirely of butter. I was hungry but didn't eat very much of it. It tasted as awful as it looked. I spent the rest of the evening sitting in front of a television, feeling a gnawing sense of hunger.

My body was so used to being awake that it didn't seem likely I'd be able to sleep. The bed felt too much like hospital. A soft green plasticy mattress covered by crisp white sheets, stamped with NSW Health in blue lettering. Nothing about it put me at ease, so I decided to remake the bed on the floor.

As I lay there, eyes closed on the brink of sleep, I realised I hadn't flossed my teeth. Floss was on the list of outlawed items along with shoelaces and anything sharp or pointy, and as such, it had been quarantined in my locker. Locker items were only accessible between 10.30-11.00 am.

But I really wanted to floss my teeth. Something about flossing felt really important, it was like a zit that once I realised it was there, I couldn't stop touching. Surely, they could make an exception to locker hours. Flossing was healthy after all.

So I walked down the still very bright hallway in my pyjamas to the Nurses' Station, a big counter in the middle of the ward that was sectioned off from patient access. In my most polite, all-girls Catholic school voice I asked the nurse if I could please have the floss from my locker.

She didn't respond, she just stood there looking me up and down. My tank top without a bra. My pyjama shorts. My bare legs and feet. She wore exactly the same expression as the mean girl at a high school party.

'Could you put a jumper on?'

'Excuse me?'

'Could you put a jumper on? It's quite inappropriate. Your

outfit. There are men around.' She placed a hand on my arm.

I stepped backwards in shock.

It was too much, I was living here, why shouldn't I be able to wear pyjamas at 8.30 at night? Were the male brains here so sex-focused that a young woman walking down a corridor in pyjamas would make it impossible for them to resist the temptation to jack off right there on the spot?

That's when I cried.

Well, actually, first I screamed. About how little sleep I'd had, and how tired I was and how as a society we really needed to raise our expectations of men.

Ten minutes and a jumper later, another adult woman stood beside me while I flossed each gap between my teeth.

When I was done, I handed the dangerous item back to her on a paper towel.

She took the paper towel, scrunched it up and put it in the bin next to me. The one act of defiance she could offer.

The next morning they needed a fasting blood test, so I couldn't eat breakfast. My body clock was scheduled to eat my bowl of yogurt and muesli at 4.39am, so by the time the blood-taking nurse arrived at ten to nine I was very hungry.

She recoiled at the sight of the now golf-ball sized bruise from the previous blood test at RPA. 'She didn't do a very good job there, now did she?'

I felt this was too harsh, the nurse at RPA had apologised three times for the multiple attempts she'd made with the needle. After the second time, she'd even offered to go and get someone else. But I didn't say any of this to the new nurse, I just smiled at her meekly and let her get to work on filling her four little vials with my blood.

Once, the blood test was over there were more tests to be done. An ECG machine was wheeled in to check my heart function. The nurse then checked my eyes and tested the reflexes of various different parts of my body.

After about half an hour she was finished with the tests. Another nurse entered the room.

'April, I have your medicine here.'

What medicine? No one had mentioned medicine to me. It must be a mistake, some mix up between me and another patient.

'I don't think those are for me,' I said, as the nurse reached me holding a little cup of pills.

'This is what the admission team wants you to take,' the nurse replied firmly.

'But what are they?' I was looking down at the pills. I was only here to fix up my sleep and I'd slept for nine hours last night. I felt fine.

'Seroquel. Abilify. Alprazolam,' she said, indicating to each of the little pills as she said their name.

'What will they do?' I was beginning to freak out slightly. I didn't like the idea of blindly putting things into my body without knowing what the effects would be.

'They'll keep you calm. Make you feel better.'

'I have to take them, don't I?'

'Yes. You do.'

So I swallowed them. But they didn't make me feel better. My mind became so foggy, I was a wandering zombie. I forgot how to read a clock. Not that it seemed to matter what time it was. There was only fog in my thoughts anyway.

The next morning a new nurse approached me. She was bright and chirpy.

'Hi April, I'm Maya. April and May that's neat! I'll be your nurse for today. If you need anything you can talk to me. The other nurses working today are Selma and Jim. There are lots of things to do here. We have a Wii that we play in the afternoon and once you get leave, there's a pool you can visit.'

I nodded along politely with her explanation. I wanted to like her but there was something about her manner that felt false, as though she wasn't really convinced that what she was saying was all that great. She looked me over for a second, then tugged my arm so I was standing close enough to hear a rushed whisper.

'Jim likes to take the girls to the pool. He likes to see them in their swimsuits. Stay away from him.'

'Okay,' I said slowly. 'I'm going outside for some air.'

'Okay,' Maya was back to her chirpy pitch. Her demeanour didn't match at all with what she'd just told me. 'I'll come find you with your medication later.'

I went outside, mulling over what Maya had just said. It had never occurred to me that people would join the medical profession for nefarious reasons. Maybe Maya was misreading the situation? Blowing a small thing she'd seen out of proportion. What if she's not said another more insistent voice. What if there's something to be frightened of in this place you're stuck in? Or someone.

18

The Invisible Hairtie

The next day the doctors were ready to see me. There were two doctors, one that asked the questions and the other that took detailed notes in a loopy scrawl. They introduced themselves and I almost immediately forgot their names.

'So, April, why are you here?'

Why am I here? That's a very good question, Doctor. I didn't want to be here. I wanted to take a drug that knocked me for out three days straight, so I could catch up on the sleep I'd missed. Then go out and deal with my life. But I'd been here for four days, and although I'd been given a lot of drugs, none of them had induced the kind of sleeping coma I wanted.

'I couldn't sleep.'

'Why not?'

A muddled, garbled version of the story poured out of me. Mixed with gossip, lies and rumours were some things I knew to be true. Someone had been having me followed, had been hacking my phone and my laptop, had gone through my room. My friends weren't really my friends. They had been pretending to care about me, while gossiping behind my back, or worse, passing information to the Someone at the centre of this.

I don't know what I was expecting the doctors to say or do with my messy, unprovable story. Maybe in that moment I just wanted sympathy. A hug or a lollipop or for one of them to say I clearly wasn't crazy and that I could go home now. None of those things happened. Instead came the verdict.

'Keep her on the Alprazolam and the Quetiapine and titrate the Abilify up to 50mg.'

It left me feeling as though I'd had a sharp comb pulled through my thoughts and something in them had been deemed unsatisfactory. I was playing a chess match, without knowing the rules. I think if they had actually said the words sleep deprived and delusional to me, I would have understood. But I didn't understand because I couldn't see what they were seeing.

My parents visited me of course. Almost every day. It always felt like our relationship was on display for all to see. They didn't feel like my parents, they felt like weird robot props who could only say lines like:

'It's so good to see you.'

'How are you feeling?'

All of the familiarity, all of the inside jokes and any type of connection I felt to them seemed as though it had been sucked from the air between us. There was a gap. A distance between us. It was not a gap I could close with words or explanation. They had their lives that went on outside of the hospital walls. And I had mine bounded by two corridors and the small outdoor grass area with a high green fence.

When these two existences collided, I tried desperately not to be cold and unfeeling, but everything about my relationship with them felt performative, as though it could be bottled down to a formula. Hug one. Hug two. Here's some food we brought for you. Here are some more clothes.

Do you need anything else? No? Okay… well you'll let us know won't you? You can call us anytime.

This was technically not true. Phone hours were only between 9.30 and 4.30 when they had plentiful staff available to monitor all the calls. There was a little yellow sign above the phone that read, 'All calls may be monitored.' Besides that the location of the phone in the middle of the common area meant that along with the staff member who listened discreetly in the pod room with the computers, anyone who happened to be watching television could also hear anything you said.

I didn't point this out to them. Everything that distressed me about being in the hospital was better left unsaid. I'd always sheltered my parents from uncomfortable truths. Even as a child I'd never liked making them unhappy. I sensed that my being here was enough strain for them to carry.

My hands shook too much to eat cereal, but I put on my best smile the minute they walked through the door.

The environment was artificial. There were beds, and food, showers and toilets, but it wasn't really living. It was existing with no real purpose. Devoid of any task to complete I sat saturated in the mess of my own thoughts. I was increasingly frustrated with nowhere to express it. No outlet in which to pour my mind's contents. I couldn't write in the notebook my parents had brought for me. Well, I could but this in itself was infuriating because the tremor in my hands reduced my handwriting to a kindergarten level.

'Are you depressed, April?' a nurse asked me on my fourth day. I'd been staring at the cereal in front of me for at least five minutes.

'No, but this place,' I gestured around me, 'is making me want to kill myself. I can't even have a hair tie because god forbid I'd use it to hang myself.'

'April, you can't talk like that here. It's distressing for other patients.'

Mentioning suicide on a mental health ward is one of those unwritten rules. Something you just don't do. No one explicitly tells you these rules until you break them.

'What can I say then? That it's a pleasure to be here and I'm having the time of my life?'

'No. No one is asking you to lie about how you feel. Just keep in mind how what you say affects the feelings of the other patients here.'

'Yeah. Of course. I'm sorry. God forbid someone offs themselves with an invisible hair tie.'

It was a bratty thing to say and one I didn't entirely mean but she had caught me at exactly the wrong moment. The pulp of my frustrations had been juiced like an orange and I had zero patience left for this nurse and her nosy questions.

There's a funny paradox about mental hospitals. They're made with the express purpose of making people feel better. A lofty aim and one that at least in my experience they rarely meet. Because when you think about it they are a prison. They may be painted in soothing colours and offer pamphlets on self-improvement but when you get down to it there's still a lock on the door, a high fence and reheated food that looks as though it was made by the most unhappy chef in existence.

And the thing about people living in prisons is it makes real life, life outside that place feel strange and foreign. Over time, your ability to live in the real world gets eroded. So, you could come out in a worse place than you were to begin with.

19

The Note in the Trashcan

Sometime later that day, I went to the bathroom. It was the one beside my bedroom. As I was drying my hands with a disposable paper towel, I looked down at the trashcan. There was nothing in it but a screwed up bit of paper. But it wasn't the faded yellow of a paper towel. It was white. It stood out against the black insides of the bin. I can't tell you what made me do it, but I put my hand into the bin and picked up the screwed up ball of paper and unfolded it. In a pink marker pen someone had written LOCK YOUR DOOR.

Holding the note in my hands, I went back to my room.

I scanned my surroundings. Yes, little things were out of place. Moved or shifted slightly. As though someone had gone through them. My stomach dropped. I didn't want someone going through my stuff. This room was the only place that was solely mine. I would get to the bottom of this. Make it clear this wasn't okay.

I practically ran to the nurses' station.

'You searched my room?' My voice was high and angry.

'April. Calm down.'

'It says it right here. That I should be locking my door. I don't want you going through my stuff, it's an invasion of my privacy.'

'April. You have to understand it's procedure when someone mentions suicide to search their room.'

'That... that was a joke. A bad joke.'

'Regardless, we had to do it for your safety.'

'No. You don't understand, I don't feel safe here anymore. And that doesn't even matter because there's nothing you can fucking do about it is there?'

'April, calm down. This isn't helping you.'

'No! This isn't helping me! You *must* see that.'

After my outburst I went back to my room to calm down. I threw my pillow against the wall until my arms were shaking from the exertion. I sat down on my bed and cried. For five minutes I allowed myself permission to wallow in the injustice of everything that surrounded me. How was I meant to act normal when everything that made me feel normal had been taken away?

What I didn't realise until I left my room was that there was a flow on effect of my screaming at the nurses. It had triggered someone else who had been spiralling since he'd arrived earlier that morning. At first, he hadn't known where he was or why he been brought to this place. He said he had been picked up off the street by the police, put in a van and brought here. No one had told him why he was being arrested.

As I walked back up the corridor to the communal dining area I could see that he was having a screaming match of his own with another nurse.

'Either tell me why the fuck I'm here or let me leave!'

'I can't give you that information right now,' replied the nurse, from behind the counter of the nurses' station. In the fishbowl room behind the glass, another nurse was watching the exchange while on the phone. Her brows were furrowed.

Things began to happen quickly after that. Within the space of the next ten minutes two police officers arrived. They had black uniforms and padded vests. Federal Police was printed in silver block letters across their shoulder blades. They approached the man who had been arguing with the nurse.

'Hey mate, you need to come with us.' He immediately stepped backwards away from them, the confusion written all across his face.

'What? Why?' he said, his voice thin and high.

I looked from the nurses, to the other patients who were all frozen watching the exchange. I realised I was waiting for someone to step in, to say it was clearly a mistake or for the officers to explain why they were there. But neither of these things happened.

The first officer took another step towards the man, closing the distance between them. He reached out to grab for the man's arm. Again, he filched back out of the officer's reach.

'Don't touch me!'

He glanced around the room desperately looking for a way out of the situation. Or for someone to come to his aid. His eyes fell on me, standing alone in the entrance of the room. I will never forget the way he looked at me. It was as though I was the only life raft in an empty ocean. Something about those pleading eyes made me call across the room.

'Stop!' The two officers turned to look me. The dismissal on their faces was clear, even from across the room. They turned back to the man.

'I mean it. Stop. Look at him. He's terrified. This is the worst day of his life. He doesn't have any idea why he's here. Or why you're here. This is the scariest moment of his life. Read him his rights for god's sake. Let him know what he's accused of and where he's going and you won't have to drag him out of here.'

I still don't know what made me say it. I guess I just knew I was seeing a real injustice in front of me and that if I didn't speak up for this stranger nobody else would.

After I finished speaking, the officer turned back to the man and said. 'Toby Michelson, you have been charged with the murder of Corey Fleming.'

They didn't say you have the right to remain silent. Or you have the right to an attorney. Or any of the things I'd been taught to expect from watching people get arrested on TV. They just put him in handcuffs and began escorting him towards the door.

When he drew level with where I was standing he stopped and looked at me.

The officer made a motion designed to hurry him along.

'Wait!' he said. 'I want to ask her a question.'

'Let him,' I said to the officer.

'What will it be like?'

'Prison? I don't know,' I began. 'I've never been there. My mum has though, she used to work there as a doctor. I imagine it's like a small city. There are good people and bad people just like in the real world. You'll find there's people there who are not unlike you.'

That was the entirety of our exchange. After that he was towed out of the hospital by the police officers and I never saw him again. I think about it a lot though. Still, to this day there is no doubt in my mind that he was framed for a crime that he did not commit.

20

The Wall

The next day I did something I am not proud of. I stand by most of my actions in this story even though at times I know they make me seem childish, bratty and naive. This is something I cannot defend or pretend is okay. I was in no immediate danger and yet I dialled 000.

It was not an emergency but I couldn't think of what else to do. On one level I understood that I was in hospital because I had not been sleeping and thus had not been thinking clearly. What I could not comprehend is how they had the right to keep me there, feeding me what seemed like an endless supply of pills. The basic premise that underpins the Mental Health Act in Australia eluded my comprehension. Primarily because in my mind sleep was my one and only problem. If I slept, I shouldn't need the pills. The doctors didn't see it this way. And I needed someone who would listen to me. So I did what you are taught to do in an emergency. I called triple zero.

As I sat down to make my call, my hands were shaking. A yellow cardboard sign sticky taped to the wall above the phone read, 'All calls made by patients may be monitored.' That didn't seem very fair to me but I put it aside and pressed the buttons anyway.

A robotic voice crackled through the speakers.

'You have dialed emergency triple zero. Please state which service you require — ambulance, police or fire?'

'Police,' I said in my clearest voice.

'Connecting you now,' the voice replied.

There was a pause and some beeping.

'Please tell me about the nature of your emergency,' said a woman's voice.

'I'm being held here against my will.' I blurted out. 'They won't let me leave. I need the police.'

'Where are you located?' asked the voice. She sounded alert.

I truly didn't know where I was. In that moment I couldn't even remember the name of the hospital. Let alone what street it was on.

'I don't know, can't you see that? Can't you track where I am?'

'I need you to confirm your location,' said the voice patiently.

'I'm in a hospital. I don't know what it's called, I can't remember.'

'Okay stay on the line with me. What's your name?'

'April. Please send the police. I need to get out of here. They keep feeding me pills and—'

At that moment the call was disconnected. A nurse's voice came through the line.

'April, you can't do that. If you do it again, you won't be allowed to use the phone.'

I slammed down the phone. My hands were shaking, this time in anger. I screamed at the phone.

'I hate you! You can't do this!'

Why couldn't I call and ask for help? Nothing I'd said had been a lie. It was all true.

I see now that the call itself was a mistake. But at the time, all I could do was cry.

When my tears turned to hiccups, I clicked my Ugg boots together three times. I even said the words under my breath.

'There's no place like home. There's no place like home. There's no place like home,' I whispered, shutting my eyes tightly. Hoping against all reasonable logic that I would open my eyes and be sitting on my bed in the middle of my bedroom, before all of this had ever happened. Worrying about my macroeconomics homework.

I opened my eyes.

Nothing had changed of course. I was still exactly where I had been sitting next to the phone cubicle in the hallway of some hospital somewhere.

That day I decided there were essentially two types of nurses. There were those nurses who thought of their profession as a calling. They went above and beyond even what was expected of them. They saw the hospital as a second home, a place that brought satisfaction and meaning to their lives. Then there was the other type of nurse who saw nursing simply as a job. A payback. This nurse was content to do the minimum required.

It might surprise you that this was the type of nurse I preferred interacting with. I found that the less caring of the two required less pretending on my part. We shared a mutual understanding that we'd both rather be somewhere else. That ticking the appropriate boxes was good enough.

'How are you feeling?'

The question came that afternoon from the first type of nurse. I paused and thought for a moment before responding.

'You don't have to do that,' I said to her.

'Do what?'

'The caring stuff.'

'That's my job,' she replied. The conviction of her feelings clear was in her voice.

'Isn't your job just to ensure that those pills go down my throat?' I asked her.

I didn't mean to offend her, but I watched as her eyes went a little watery.

'That's a part of it, yes,' she replied 'But it isn't the whole job. Now, how are you feeling?'

'Fine.'

I didn't really feel fine. I felt miserable. But there's something about being asked constantly whether or not I was okay that had made me pull my emotions in. Squash them down and try to hold them as close as I could. How I really felt was a secret I kept to myself now.

Taking the hint that I didn't want to talk, she let me go back to writing in my notebook.

'Do you mind if I sit?'

This time I was looking up at a man with floppy brown hair. He was wearing a polo shirt, but not the expensive kind you buy at Ralph Lauren, the kind that sit in the sales bins at Best & Less, a pair of khaki shorts and no shoes. He seemed nice enough;

I was starting to get bored of scribbling in my notebook, so I replied, 'No, please,' and indicated to the chair across from mine. 'Are you new?' I asked him.

'Yeah. Last night.'

'Welcome to hell,' I said, my voice laced with sarcasm.

'Don't worry. I know,' he replied cheerily as though being brought here didn't bother him in the slightest.

'Have you been here before?' I asked.

'Yep.'

'Why did you come back?' I genuinely wanted to know the answer to this. In my opinion the food alone was enough to make anyone not want to make a return visit.

'I didn't have much choice in the matter,' a note of bitterness creeping into his voice.

'Me neither,' I said. 'I mean it's my first time but I'd much rather be somewhere else right now.'

'I walked around this whole place this morning,' he told me carefully, lowering his voice slightly.

'Yeah?'

'I nearly jumped the fence.'

Something about those words 'jumped the fence' rattled around in my head even hours after the conversation ended.

This brings me to the wall.

I will say that before this I hadn't even remotely considered an escape attempt. But that afternoon it became all I could think about. As far as escape attempts go, it wasn't a serious or well-planned one. I remember sitting under a point where a solid brick wall was built next to the fence to offer some shade and thinking I could climb that. That wall isn't that high and the bench leaning against the wall is a leg up. It would be easy to climb.

The hard bit would be getting down on the other side. A straight two metre drop onto concrete. But what was that really, a grazed knee, if I was really unlucky a rolled ankle? I'd rolled my ankle before. I could take it.

I scanned my surroundings. No one else was even outside. The perfect opportunity to strike. I looked back at the wall. Maybe this would make them take my requests to leave more seriously. Something about that misguided thought prompted me into action. It took less than thirty seconds before I was sitting on top of the wall. Sitting up there I froze. I'd never been scared of heights but the ground looked further away from this angle and the concrete below infinitely more perilous. And where to run to?

That falter. That moment of indecision about jumping

down was all the time that was needed for a nurse to look up from inside and see me.

Then came the cries of she's on the wall. They rushed outside and the process of pulling me down with some degree of safety began. In the end, I was made to climb down onto a chair, and then herded inside like a misbehaving animal.

The relief of the nurses was palpable. Chatter of I can't believe that just happened and good thing we caught her, good thing she's not hurt rang in the air around me.

I barely listened to the reprimand and the you shouldn't have done that, April. In my head, I was still caught in that moment of decision. I was still screaming at myself internally to JUMP and RUN. I hadn't though. In fact, all I'd really achieved was to increase the level of surveillance that the nurses were required to perform on me. It hadn't been the bold act of protest that would finally make them take me seriously. It was merely interpreted as the desperation of a childish nuisance who had been stretched to the end of her rope.

21

The Chapter That Feels Fake

Eventually, after my attempt to climb the wall, I settled into my new life. Somewhat accepting of the circumstances that surrounded me. I looked for answers to my biggest questions. Who had sent all the real patients on cruises? Who was paying these actors to pretend to be mentally unwell? How did they know so much about me?

The other "patients" were hesitant to speak to me about most of these things. It seemed they'd signed contracts that prevented them opening up honestly to me. My answers came in little dribbles of information, guessing games and riddles.

They had been preparing for this admission, my admission, for almost a year. They joked they had been to April University. I asked what they had studied at April University. All about you came the reply. I believed them. Because they did know stuff about me that you could only know having spent serious time following me. Stalking me. When I cried, they offered me make-up wipes, the same brand I had used every day on the train after uni. They knew what courses I'd taken in my HSC year. They asked questions about my major work for Extension English. I asked if they had read it. We wanted to, came the response. One of your teachers was going to sell us a copy. But the principal put her foot down.

For all intents and purposes it was like moving into the Big Brother House with ten strangers who knew almost everything about you.

My main question was who was funding this? Who was at the top? Who had spent this much money studying me? We can't tell you that, they replied. We really wish we could. But we promised.

You promised? I queried them. Like signed an NDA?

Yes, came the answer.

But I could still guess? And you could say yes or no? They looked warily at each other.

So began the guessing game.

The riddle was this. Their first name has another meaning. Their middle name is a team teenage girls like to join. Their last name is a creature that swims in the ocean, and something a baker makes.

I puzzled through the answers to the riddle for a few minutes with them. Eventually, they acknowledged that I'd gotten all the answers right.

I was still confused. I don't know anyone with that name I said.

At this they laughed. He knows you, they said.

Did it creep me out? Yes it did. But the whole situation was so beyond the point of creepy that it lost all of the uncomfortableness that usually surrounds creepy things. This was a new world. We had passed the point of no return. In this new construct of reality, I just wanted to talk to this person. I wanted their side of the story. That's what lead me to Rosemary.

Rosemary was another "patient". Her entire purpose seemed to be to sit in a chair and report on everything that I did under her breath. I gravitated toward her initially because of her direct and unmonitored connection with the outside world. I wanted to speak to whoever was on the other end of her earpiece.

I sat down in an armchair across from her and tried to make sense of what she was muttering to the person on the other end of her earpiece. At least I was pretty sure at this stage it was an earpiece, I'd heard enough snatches of what sounded like one side of a conversation to believe that she wasn't simply muttering to herself as an act. She had stopped muttering and was now looking very intently at me.

'Are you okay?'

I was struck by the gentleness with which she asked the question. I didn't know what to say, eventually deciding on a noncommittal answer. 'Sort of, I guess.' Then I asked the question I'd been dying to know the answer to. 'Who are you whispering to all the time?'

'Do you want to talk to him?' Rosemary asked.

'Yes!' I replied with instant conviction. Of course I wanted to talk to him. I wanted answers to my many questions.

'He's listening,' Rosemary replied. 'What would you like to say?'

I decided to go for my most pressing question first. 'How does he know me? Like have we ever met?'

As Mark explained who he was, faint memories of the night when I was fourteen trickled back into my head. The boy from Omegle, that night when it felt like my whole life was over, the sweet, kind boy who had listened to me talk for hours. I hadn't thought about him in years. But he wasn't a stranger. He did know me in a way.

It was an odd way to communicate with someone. Rosemary repeated what Mark was saying to her through the earpiece. So, it was like having a conversation through a conduit, Rosemary was speaking for Mark. It was his words but I heard them in her voice.

He asked me if I was angry with him, for what he had done. I thought about it deeply.

'In the beginning, I wanted to know everything. I wanted an itemised list of who told you stuff about me. All the invasions of my privacy that you made. I wanted to know it all. Now, having met you, or re-met you and now that I know who you are, I don't want those things as much. I guess when I realised, like when I saw all the pieces fitting together and the picture they were making I made a decision to come here, to a hospital and get help with my life. Not to go to a police station, which I did consider. But I didn't think that would help me.'

He apologised after that. Profusely. And he explained, 'To start with I just wanted to know you. Then the more I learnt the more I wanted to make your life easier. It seemed like you were trying so hard with everything.'

I interrupted him, 'But you realise by doing that, you've only made a mess of it, my life I mean. I mean look where I am.'

'Yes, I see that and I'm sorry.'

After that it felt like we'd signed a peace treaty of sorts, the tone of the conversation changed. Mark asked me if there was anything he could do to help. My first instinct was to say I think you've done quite enough already, don't you? But I held back from that, I thought about it. 'I guess the main thing I'm struggling with is feeling useless. My normal life is so full and busy. I hate sitting around all day.'

'Do you mind if I try and help you with that?'

This question surprised me, in my head, the person who had ruined my life, who had sent all the sick people from the hospital, like you clean week-old takeout from a fridge could only be malicious and self-centred. This did not compute with the version of Mark I was experiencing when I was actually talking with him. I turned my attention to the question, what would help me?

'Bring me difficult problems to try and solve. People who are in distress and need help. I'd like to do some good while I'm here.'

I don't know what exactly I was expecting but it probably wasn't anything like what followed. Mark delivered on his promise to help me.

I'm going to recount these days I spent with Rosemary and Mark the best I can. Essentially they boil down to this — from two armchairs in the corridor of a hospital— Rosemary, Mark and I solved problems.

It went like this, Mark would travel to the person with the problem, and I would either talk to them directly via Rosemary's earpiece, or so I didn't look like I was talking to myself, Rosemary would recount what the caller was saying and I would talk to her, my voice picked up by the hidden button-shaped microphone attached to her blouse.

I doubt you will believe the list of people whose problems we tackled. It would seem far-fetched, deranged and crazy if I were to name them. Because this technically needs to be fiction, for reasons that I will explain in the following chapters, I've decided to give these people aliases. I myself signed no NDAs or legal documents that would prevent me from naming them outright. But something about that feels slimy and uncomfortable to me and selfishly I want this book to be more about me than an exercise in name-dropping other people.

For you, I'm sure the question of why will come up a lot. Why did so many of these people agree to or seek out meetings with me? Am I really that special? Was my advice truly that groundbreaking? I think the answer had a lot to do with the team of people around me. And the philosophy of wanting to do as much good as possible in what became a limited time frame.

Portrait Girl was one of the first people I remember helping. Portrait Girl, as her name suggests, had her portrait painted by a prominent artist, who had then entered that portrait into a competition and subsequently won that competition. What happened next was the reason for Portrait Girl's distress, the portrait which showed Portrait Girl naked had been plastered on the front page of a newspaper without Portrait Girl's consent. This choice of the newspaper had meant that Portrait Girl had received a slew of unsolicited messages from complete strangers commenting on her naked body and her choices. Portrait Girl was feeling used and overwhelmed.

I felt bad for Portrait Girl instantly. I saw the injustice of it. The problem was that technically nothing that had happened was illegal. Yet, I still felt like Portrait Girl deserved some form of compensation for the emotional labour that the media conglomerate had foisted onto her shoulders. What we did next was slightly sneaky.

We contacted a producer at a television game show of said media conglomerate. We explained we had a contestant for the show. We then proceeded to rig the game show, so that Portrait Girl was able to win a sum of money and thus walk away with compensation from said media conglomerate. I can honestly say I don't feel even one tiny ounce of guilt about the whole arrangement.

Some of the things we worked on were a relatively small scale like Portrait Girl. Others were much larger. Then there were things we were asked to do that we didn't. The big secret event was the first of these things. The big secret event was taking place in a government war room. At the time we learnt of its occurrence, we had a large enough profile that they offered to let us sit in on what was taking place. This was not the kind of invitation that was offered lightly. But everyone who was qualified to sit in that room either by being elected to that position or by serving in the service of their country for a great length of time was already in the room. I didn't feel like we had any right to be there. So, we politely declined.

The next call came from a Newsroom, or rather it came from the head of a news organisation. He was fishing for information about the big secret event, all of his journalists were currently at a party, but he had been hearing rumblings that something big was happening, did I know anything about it? Yes I did, and without telling him what it was, my advice was that his newsroom leave that party, go back to their office and be ready to break something big in the next few hours.

What followed over that time were several conversations between the head of the news organisation and myself. Could they use me as a source to confirm the story? No, not unless they wanted their credibility called into question. Could I confirm something they had from another source? I mean yes, on background, that information was correct but they still needed another source to confirm. They couldn't use me. The conversation went back and forth until they had enough confirmation to break the story. I was thanked by the head of the news organisation and signed off the call. The next day *The New York Times* wrote a short piece praising how well the news organisation had handled the coverage of the big secret event.

I can't capture everything that took place in these meetings. Nor recall everyone I met with. That day, we also spoke to a guy who was teaching rap to underprivileged youth about casting a musical. Took a meeting in London about promising TV pilots and film scripts that producers felt had slipped through the cracks and tried to connect them with funding sources. It was a whirlwind of creativity, joy and passion and to this day it contains some of the best moments of my life. I don't want to paint it as all sunshine and rainbows because there were some truly hard moments as well.

One of these was the two calls with the Distressed Boyfriend. The Distressed Boyfriend was a very public figure. Someone famous due to the weight of their last name. I was for some reason more starstruck speaking with the Distressed Boyfriend than I had been at any point prior to this.

I opened the conversation by telling him, 'I think I know who I'm speaking to but I don't know what I'm supposed to call you. How to address you.'

'You can call me whatever you want. Honestly, I don't care.'

That wasn't much of a directive to go off, so I went with what would make me the most comfortable and suggested, 'Okay why don't we skip the formalities and just use first names.'

He agreed to this. Then I asked him what I could help with.

'Well, I really hope you can help me. Everyone I've spoken to says you're very good with problems, somewhat of a miracle worker and I'm certainly in need of one those.'

'I don't know who you've spoken to, but I'm not a miracle worker. I listen and I try to offer the best solution I can. Why don't you start from the beginning?'

Distressed Boyfriend explained that the problem he was experiencing was that a few hours ago, his fiancee had shared with him that she was feeling suicidal. I understood then why Mark had been reluctant to let me speak with Distressed Boyfriend. What could I really say to him that would make a difference? If something bad were to happen could I handle having this on my conscience? I couldn't think about those things though. I had to put them to one side and just try to help Distressed Boyfriend the best I could.

I asked some questions around the nature of what Distressed Boyfriend's fiancee had said to him. I quickly came to the conclusion that things in his life could not continue as they were. I asked Distressed Boyfriend what he valued more, his relationship or his position in public life? I said I didn't see that there was a way that he could feasibly keep them both. He was very firm that the relationship was what he valued more. I made some suggestions around a way he could take some strategic steps back from his public life.

When Distressed Boyfriend called me for the second time, I was using Rosemary's phone connection to speak to a friend. I was reluctant to hang up the call, as this friend had become somewhat of a refuge for me. I usually spoke to her at the end of these crazy days as a way to detox from their heaviness.

When I answered, Distressed Boyfriend was in a panic. He had forgotten that he and his fiancee were scheduled to attend an event that evening. The car had just arrived and neither of them were ready. Distressed Boyfriend was trying to insist that given how she was feeling his fiancee obviously shouldn't go to the event. She was insisting that they had already agreed to go and thus must attend.

I imagined her, this hurting but determined woman putting on a dress she didn't feel comfortable in and reapplying powder to her nose. In a former life, she had been an actress. I explained to Distressed Boyfriend that what she was doing was applying warpaint and battle amour in order to face the barrage of media and photographers that were now a core ingredient of their life together. This was not something she wanted to do, but it was something she felt she had to do.

At first, he tried to argue with me. Surely, this wasn't the time. I explained that this was like being a soldier in the military, that the makeup and the pretty dress were like the combat uniform he had worn. That continuing to argue the point would be fruitless. The command had been issued. They had called for places on the film set. The best thing that he could do would be to go with her, hold her hand and not let go.

Most of the people who we met with I liked, at least to some degree. There is one consequence that I do feel conflicted over.

Mark was leaving a meeting with an American company, when we were approached by one of their employees. The man informed us that he had been instructed under no circumstances to speak to us outside of the meeting room. That because we had not signed on to work exclusively with that company and were actively taking assignments with the competition, all the employees had been instructed that were they to even speak to us outside of the meeting room, or they risked being terminated.

'Why have you approached us then?' I asked through my earpiece.

'Because I'm desperate. I wasn't even supposed to be at this meeting. I've been on leave for a month now because my daughter is in the hospital with anorexia. She's well… she's dying. Anyway, I wasn't supposed to be here but I got a call this morning saying if I didn't come today I'd lose my job. So I'm here. And I'm speaking to you because, because I've never seen anything like that. I've never heard anyone articulate so clearly everything that's wrong with our industry. And you have this reputation as somewhat of a miracle worker. So, I'm asking you to please come with me, and try to save my daughter.'

After he finished speaking I asked for a moment with Mark to discuss it all. My first question was whether Mark felt comfortable getting in a car with this stranger to go to the hospital. It was clear that this was something Mark wanted to do. So we pushed back the other meetings that we had scheduled, Mark got in the car and was driven to the hospital.

I didn't exactly have a plan as to what we were going to do or say when we got there. As you will know, somewhere between the age of fourteen and fifteen I'd had a pretty nasty eating disorder of my own. So I understood the mentality. It had never been as bad as this girl's though. When we arrived the doctors we spoke to suggested that she had hours not days left.

The girl was drifting in and out of consciousness in a dream-like state. I don't know where exactly this idea came from but some kind of gut instinct told me it was the right call. I had Mark enter the room alone.

'Who are you?' asked a feeble voice through the phone. I only ever heard her voice. To this day, I still have no idea what she looks like.

'Death,' Mark replied at my instruction.

'Oh.'

'You must have been expecting me. You're very very close now,' Mark repeated the words to her as I said them.

'What's it like?'

'I don't know. I have never died. It's not that different from falling asleep, you let go and you're no longer here.'

'Does it hurt?'

'No, not usually. I'm going to offer you the choice though — you can go to sleep now and let go, or you can hold on and when you wake up you can fight.'

After that she lost consciousness, and Mark waited at the hospital with her family. The doctors were puzzled by what happened next for when she woke up she was stronger. She began to swallow water. Mark told me that her family and the doctors looked at him as though he had performed some sincere act of magic.

We kept updated with the girl's family and in the days that followed she continued to make strides.

I feel conflicted sharing these stories with you, because in the majority of cases I didn't get the privilege of knowing how they ended. In some cases also, I didn't want to pretend I had more impact than I did. I know the term miracle worker was thrown around a bit in this chapter and I feel guilty about even writing that, because the reality is I was just a girl trying to do some good in the world.

This is partly why I called this 'the chapter that feels fake'. I couldn't choose to edit around this chapter though because it is necessary to understand what follows.

22

Another Chapter I Did Not Want to Write

Writing these chapters has been like pulling out my own teeth. Not because I'm not proud of the work that Rosemary, Mark and I did. I am. Immensely so. But rather because I feel incredibly conflicted about sharing the parts of this story that are not my own. The following two stories are the ones I feel most reluctant to write down.

In the first, I am terrified that the subject will recognise herself and resent me for writing it. Not that I intend to write an unflattering portrait of her. But she has already been put under so much scrutiny, been critiqued in so many ways that I feel another account will only add to the noise. Which is not something I want to do.

The person I speak of was someone I spoke to three or four times over the week that this chapter takes place within. She was a musician. Naturally, most of our conversation revolved around words, fragments of prose or poetry that she then developed into song lyrics. This process of storytelling was something I found immensely rewarding. But at one point in the conversation she stopped me mid-sentence to ask me a question.

'April, your words are so beautiful, you paint with them.

And I— I don't feel…like all I do is talk shit with my friends. You could have a poetry book with all this material.'

'You feel like I'm wasting it if I give it to you.'

'Yes!'

'Let me tell you something, I could have a poetry book if I wanted one. I don't though. It would sell eight copies. And seven of those would be bought by my mother. I'd much rather have you turn these words into music. People will actually hear them that way.'

I was so sure of those words when I spoke them. I didn't want or need to be named a co-writer on her songs. I didn't think I deserved that. All I was doing was picking up shinny rocks and shells from a beach and handing them to her. She was the one fashioning them into jewellery. Into pieces of art in their own right.

It makes for an interesting experience listening to those songs now with other people though. I'm always holding myself back from saying, I helped write that you know. I know the full story behind that song you're singing along to.

The final story about her I want to share is something she did for me. Towards the end of our conversations she asked if there was anything she could do for me to say thank you. I debated this for a minute and then told her about how my dad had always been the one to pick me up from primary school. He had been the only dad in the playground. Everyone else had been picked up by their mums. I asked her the next time she toured if she would go to that very same primary school and introduce herself to a dad picking up his daughter from school, walk back to their car with them and offer them concert tickets.

She agreed to this plan and a year later she pulled up to that very same primary school and did as I asked.

I tell this story because for me it illustrates everything that these days were for me. Creation for the pure joy of it. Not for any material gain or recognition. I had the luxury of making art purely for the simple pleasure of making it. Like a kid at a colouring table, I got to draw and play and then I got to present all my crazy ideas and have them taken seriously by masters of that particular craft.

The second story in this chapter is one I didn't want to write for a different reason. This is because it is the story of an organisation in a hard situation trying to do the right thing. It is the story of an organisation caught right on the edge of scandal they know is coming. They know what has happened, what will continue to happen, yet at the time I met with them they had no way of stopping it. No hard evidence with which to convict the guilty party. No means through which to cut the cancer from their system.

I felt bad for the people running this organisation because their hearts were truly in the right place. They wanted to weed out their bad apple. The pedophile that had wormed his way into a position of power within their ranks. They were stricken and disgusted by his actions. The crimes that were alleged against him.

But extracting someone from any position of power they've held for some time is never an easy task. Often, the person in question has built a system of defence around themselves. They are usually on alert for any threat.

At the time of my meeting with this organisation, they had locked their top athletes, six teenage girls in separate hotel rooms without access to their phones. Upon hearing this my first reaction was to demand that they give the girls back their mobiles immediately.

'They are teenage girls, not prisoners,' I told them. 'They have every right to text each other about this. All you're achieving is fostering a climate of more fear and mistrust.'

They agreed and the girls were given back their phones.

We talked about what would happen when the looming scandal finally broke in the media. About the best path forward being not to run away from acknowledging it. And allowing the people who had been hurt a chance to grieve, to be angry. Not a method for stuffing it into a closet and pretending it didn't happen but a true admission of guilt. If their sport was going to survive this scandal, then this was what was needed.

Mostly, I think, they took my words to heart. They cared about trying to do the right thing.

I tell this story here to show you a contrast between intentions. The story in the next chapter is not like those contained in this one. It is good set against evil. Before these experiences I never believed that they were distinct lines. I thought it all blended together inside of us.

I feel differently now. I think pure evil definitely does exist. I'm not so sure about pure good, but either way, if there is a God, I'm not sure they spend much time at their judgment desk. I think they just look out on all of it, the best and the worst of humanity with a kind of bemused pity.

23

Don't Talk About Politics

For most of my life, I've had very little interest in politics. I've followed it with the same level of interest as you follow a sport you don't know the rules of. It's always been something that was on the periphery of my attention.

The thing about the work that Mark and I were doing though is that it started to attract attention from smaller and then more significant political operations. And the more of these meetings we took, the more others requested us. This is the story of how Mark ended up sitting across the table from someone we both loathed. Someone that we were instructed to avoid at all costs.

I've debated a lot about whether I can put his name on paper. It's a real name, as real as yours or mine and belongs to a real life, a real lineage, a real legacy. Typing his name also has some very real consequences attached to it. The scared little girl in me once toyed with the idea of writing him out of this story entirely. Of writing a different version of the truth where he was a nurse. Or a doctor. That narrative would be simpler. Cleaner.

Then there's another part of me which feels I have nothing left to lose. That wants to stand in the sun with my truth. Call this book a memoir. Build a whole media tour around blasting out what an awful person he is.

I have to find a middle ground between these two paths. This is the best one I have found.

There was a meeting. In a room. In a white building. With members of a political party. In which awful things were asked of me. In this meeting, though there were six people around the table, but only Mr. Canberra asked the questions. The questions that still haunt me. Because all the questions could be boiled down to just one.

How do we spend less on helping people?

I gave answers through gritted teeth.

At the end of the meeting a deal was struck between us. At the time, a friend said there was a name in chess for what I was doing. A queen's sacrifice.

That makes it sound brave. Noble even.

It wasn't.

I knew I was a sitting duck. An easy target. Trapped. Cornered. I knew he would seek me out either way. Try to find my Achilles heel, the point through which he could bend me to his will. Just like he had pushed and prodded the people sitting around him until he had found their weak spots. Their soft, mushy centres.

I knew all of this and I wanted some control over what he took from me. A seat at the negotiating table.

So, in a way I did agree to it. To what happens next, as much as a person can agree to a rape, I did.

The list was the last thing I did in the time before. The last thing I held in my hands.

There were almost as many names on the list as I have fingers. Names scribbled hastily in red pen. I looked at the scrappy piece of paper and saw how little the names meant to him. How he respected none of them. They meant close to nothing to him.

I also saw stories. I couldn't help it. Or flashes of stories. All muddled together. Tied by a common thread. The unwelcome touch of this man. The flash of his polaroid camera. Their names printed in red ink on this list.

I saw glimpses into the lives of these women. I saw the outfits they would never wear again. The business suits that they would push to the back of their closets. A dress that would remain in limbo, neither worn or thrown away.

I saw the tears of anger or pain cried into tissues behind the walls of a therapist's office or squashed into pillowcases late at night. I saw a gallery of hurt and embarrassment.

I saw the cost. These were smart, brilliant career women. Idealistic and shiny. I saw the words they would never speak. The jobs they would never go for. I saw how they would choose to settle for less than they deserved.

How? How? How? I asked myself. How could it go this far? How could this many women be cowed into silence?

Does it make the others sick that even after all this time, all this pain, not one of them has ever sat before a judge? That these crimes are still only whispers, only rumours, only the unspoken rule never to visit his office alone.

Are there times they regret their silence? These women with their names on the list. I knew that there were serious stakes. I knew that they had lives and reputations and families to protect. I knew there were reasons to be silent.

But were there times that they wish they'd asked more of themselves?

Was that judging them too harshly? Was I simply looking through a time portal into my own future?

I balled the list up in my fist. I put it in my mouth and swallowed it. Maybe their anger, their hurt, their pain would keep me safe in that room. Or at least I hoped it would.

24

Red Mattress Night

Between ordinary life and unthinkable violence there exists a thin but distinct line. On one side a train carriage full of commuters trundles their way to their 9 to 5s. On the other the police pick through a mess of body parts, exploded seats and fragments of broken metal. The wreckage caused by a bomb built in the bedroom of a teenage boy. Across the line again and the older sister of that teenage boy drops her daughter off at preschool and gossips to the other mothers about Love Island. In another life she spends the morning at the emergency department with a broken collarbone because her husband came home drunk and pushed her against a wall with a little too much force.

We may spend months or years never crossing close to this line. Never close enough to see how proximate those other lives are to us. And until you are forced to cross the line, you may delude yourself into thinking that it is a wall or a fence. Carefully patrolled and effective at keeping these bad things far from reach. The reality however is that there is no high wall or strong fence that runs between brutal violence and mundane existence. No dramatic crossing or deep momentous change one must make to reach one from the other. Or at least not in my experience.

The walk to the room came first. It was not a long one, less than 100 metres in length. Two locked doors. A different part of the hospital. I bounced from one foot to the next with a fountain of nervous energy. I knew what was coming from the phone call but my brain wasn't allowing me to focus on it fully. The nurse walked in front of me. When we reached the room she stood aside and let me go in. Would there be enough time to fall deeply asleep before he gets here? Could they give me an injection to knock me out? Would that be better? To not know what happened at all? And if I didn't ever wake up? If he broke his promise not to kill me? Too many questions. Think about something else.

The mattress was red. Red is an odd colour choice for a mattress. I've never seen a red mattress before. They didn't put any sheets on the bed. Probably better. Less mess to clean. Less evidence to hide. The lack of sheets made the mattress stand out. It was the kind of red that remains stained on lips even hours after its application. A high quality lipstick-red worn by flight attendants and hotel receptionists.

Red. It was the only colour in a room that otherwise looked like neutral yellow paint had been thrown over every surface. Later, the first time I wrote about it, an earlier more imagined draft of this story, a girl told me that the red mattress didn't feel very believable. That it even though the symbolism was nice, it didn't feel real. Part of me cringed as though she had slapped me. No part of this is fiction I wanted to scream.

I laid down on the bed and waited. I thought about the choices that led me here. To this moment. If I could change them now, would I choose a different path?

Then he was in the doorway and I no longer had any time left to wonder.

He filled the doorway. The whole room. I felt small again. Fragile. Breakable.

He has a Polaroid camera in his hands. He sets it down on the desk. This is his signature. He likes Polaroids. Tiny trophies. Soon, he will tell me he has many of them. A little gallery. Mementos to his destruction. The arse of a woman with red hair. The tits of a woman with blonde hair. Later he will threaten to put this polaroid on PornHub. In the moment this will scare me. Later, I will tell myself if this happens it is not a big deal.

You know what is coming. I doubt I even need to say it.

Rape.

He raped me but he did more than that. Before he penetrated he prepared my body. Ruined it. I think the legal term is grievous bodily harm. With his hands he pulled and twisted at my hip joints and my shoulders until they dislocated from their sockets. One by one each joint was pulled out of position, until I resembled a pretzel with legs floating up near my head and arms sticking out of my body at odd angles. He was slow with this. Leisurely. There was a sick gleam in his eyes. He was the kid who burns ants with a magnifying glass, and I was the ant.

There was a purpose to this of course. A rationale. He talked as he tortured me. In the animated, excited way that a kid explains their favourite cartoon, he explained everything he was going to do. The joints could be put back into place. But my body would never be the same. The quick twitch, the explosive power and control needed to land big jumps would be gone. He was almost sure, he'd even consulted with experts. In the space of mere minutes, the athletic skills I'd spent years of ice time perfecting would be gone. I would never land another axel. Never skate the same way again. He told me gleefully that if he was really lucky pain would follow me the rest of my life. I wouldn't be able to walk without it.

At first, all of this information reaches me. At first, I feel all the agony. The first hip leaving the socket is like no sensation I've ever experienced. It's excruciating. In circumstances that aren't torture, a car accident or a fall, my guess is that if a person dislocates their hip, they pretty rapidly pass out. But he couldn't have that. So he has to give me a break between each joint. A rest period. I feel each second between the first hip and the shoulder dislocation that follows. I feel another wave of pain after he walks to the other side and pulls the other shoulder. He saves the right hip for last. This is the leg that punches up to take off for an axel. The leg that let me fly.

'Say goodbye to your axel, April.'

Another spasm of agony.

Next came the trophy. He picked up the polaroid camera from the desk.

He arranged the photo meticulously. He said there was an art to taking these photos. In it were my dislocated arm and leg, an exposed left breast, his penis and my face. He twisted my arm so that there was a tear running down my cheek. He made me stare at the camera lens.

Then the fucking begins. I have been bleeding since the start of my admission. He pulled the tampon from my body. Threw it to the floor. He liked the blood. He was still talking. Something about me being wrong about him. Something about his childhood. Something about murdering his father.

I don't try to listen. I feel the pain but at the same time I am floating above the room. I am reliving images of things I love as he fucks me. I am not here. I am 12. I am listening to the exact sound a basketball makes as it shushes through the net. I am 13. And I am cantering a pony along a soft sandy trail. I am 16. And Jake is looking at me in a polka dot dress at a friend's party. Above me he is growling something. He is my King. He wants me to say it. I am 18. Eugene is picking up my red leather wallet from the ground. This is what it should always be. Flirting and butterflies. Not commands. I say it.

Repeat the words he wants to hear. My parents are smiling at me, I have just finished high school.

He puts his hands around my neck. Tightens them. My chest is burning. I just get faces now. Mum. Dad. Blaise. Albrina. Eugene. Jake. Mark. What does Mark even look like? I am seeing everyone I love most as he kills me.

A woman appears at the door. He turns and smiles at her, but does not release his fingers from my throat. I am still dying. There is no air left in my lungs. He does not stop. She begins to count down from 10.

10.

9.

8.

7.

Everything in my vision is starting to blur. I feel like I'm floating between my physical body and the ceiling of the room. Like I can choose where to be.

6.

5.

'She's going to die.'

He just laughs.

So, she counts faster.

4.

3.

2.

1.

Half. She has invented this number for my benefit. She is willing me to hold on. I don't think I can. I let go. There was a moment where I wondered whether I was dead. A moment where there was a choice. A choice to go forward, to go on, to somewhere else or go back to my broken body. Somehow I also knew that going back was the harder option. That it would be easier to cut whatever thread was still holding me in that room. This moment seemed to stretch, as though I could sit forever in the nothingness and make the decision. Sometimes, I still wonder if it was the right call to come back.

He released my neck and I coughed myself back to life. Even the smallest movement of my limbs was agony. He stood up, jumped off the bed, slid the condom off his dick and dropped it on the floor.

Then his pants were up, he fastened his belt and left the room. As he passed the window, he glanced back at me. Pride written all over his face. His new trophy in his hands.

She moved from the doorway. Straight to my dislocated limbs. I was staring at the condom on the floor. If I could have walked I would have picked it up. Got rid of it somehow.

Another woman entered and I tried to communicate this need to her. I didn't want any part of him still in the room. She got it.

The first woman barked at her to help with the realigning of my hips. Hold me down.

The second woman argued back. Look at her face, she retorted. Look at where she's looking. The second woman won the argument. She cleaned the room at a lightning pace.

'Now can we make sure she can move her toes tomorrow?'

Getting the joints back into their sockets wasn't pleasant. It required moving them from positions they had been in for 10 minutes? Had it been longer? I didn't know. But with effort and steady hands they managed it.

I just lay there staring at the ceiling. I couldn't really speak. Words wouldn't come.

The second woman asked if I'd like something to help me sleep. For the first time, since I'd been there it seemed like the medication actually had a purpose.

She left, returning with a pill and a cup of water. I swallowed gratefully. I wanted a dreamless sleep.

When the room was quiet, I pretended I was sending individual body parts to sleep. First, my toes, then my legs and arms, my torso. When at last I reached my brain, the drug was strong enough to pull me under.

25

Aftermath

I did not fuss when the nurses woke me the next morning and told me I was moving rooms. I did not fuss about walking down the corridor in pyjama pants covered in dried blood. It did not feel important. I was grateful to be able to walk. Well, not walk exactly. Hobble.

After I was moved to my new room, they immediately asked me if I wanted breakfast. I remember thinking why would I want to go to breakfast in these blood-stained clothes. I wanted a shower. I wanted a door that locked from the inside that no one could open.

They exchanged worried expressions when I refused to come and eat. As though they were being graded on their ability to keep me alive. I sat in my room silently until they left and then snuck into the bathroom and locked myself inside.

The first thing I did was study my reflection in the mirror. Looking for some perceivable difference in the bruises and the blood. I found that they were only marks and stains.

The walls around were silent. Pressing in on my terror. Holding my screams captive. Who was this strange being who'd emerged from the room with the red mattress? She didn't feel like me.

I took off my pyjamas. I put my soiled underwear into the sanitary container next to the toilet because I didn't want to look at it.

An odd pattern of bruises was appearing in different places across my body. It reminded me of a few months prior when I had dyed my hair and been left with blue-black stains on my skin where the dye had rubbed off.

The next thing I did was take a shower. There was no point keeping the evidence on my body for the rape exam that was never going to happen. The room had probably already been cleaned of my blood. At some point during the shower, I heard a nurse calling out my name. I didn't bother to reply. Eventually, when they realised I was in the bathroom, I heard fragments of a conversation.

'Should she be in there by herself?'

Should I? No one had said you can't go to the bathroom. No one had said don't take a shower. Just like no one had called the police last night.

There were no police to call. He owned them. Like he owned the building. No one had said you can't come in. Visiting hours are over. You're not on the list. There was not a room in the country he could not force his way into.

At least the bathroom door was locked. At least it was over. At least I could clean it away.

I made the water go as hot as I could. Then as cold. I scrubbed until the blood was gone. I sat down on the floor with my back against the wall and thought about never getting up. About staying under that water forever. Never moving from those tiles.

I got up. I put on clean clothes and looked at myself in the mirror again.

I read a lot of accounts of assault before ever writing my

own. I've come to the conclusion that the common experience isn't ever the assault itself. It's the moments after. The moment you're left alone in a bathroom for the first time.

The moment you can't help but feel different. Empty. As though something has been taken from you. As though some innocent part of your soul has gone. Left. Slipped right out of your chest.

I remember little of the hours and days that followed. The shock turned to numbness. The world around me felt bland as though I'd stepped into a black and white movie. The days fell into a pattern of passing time. I was not allowed back onto the old ward. So I didn't have access to Rosemary and the earpiece that had been my link to the outside world.

Mostly I tried to push everything that had happened down, out of my conscious mind but that was only half successful. I lived on the edge of panic. I found myself watching *Law and Order* in cold sweat. Waking from swirling nightmares. Always anticipating that there would be another meeting. Doubting that he would be able to stay away. That he would be able to resist the opportunity to revel in the damage he had done. The mess I had become.

This prediction turned out to be completely correct. In a way he did come back. More to gloat and congratulate himself than anything else. This time he brought two police officers with him. He delighted in telling me how I would be returning to this hospital at regular intervals to ensure that his message of ownership sunk in. He was turned on by the thrill of recounting all his crimes in front of the two police officers, who he also apparently owned.

When he was done with the gloating, he followed me back to my room. My memories of what happened in the room are patchy. My brain had turned off its capacity for feeling. Even looking back now, the experience feels neutral as though I'm watching it happen to a television character I don't particularly care about. Maybe there's only so much suffering one person can truly absorb. Maybe I had reached my limit. Anything beyond what I was already holding just became overflow.

Nobody mentioned the night with the red mattress again. And time moved on. The days became a week. I was told I would be moving to a different hospital. If there was a reason for this no one bothered to explain it to me.

The day I was departing for the new hospital arrived. I got into the van and watched a blur of different streets roll by from the window. Upon arrival I was given a room with blue walls and a broken blind that didn't move from the closed position. It was a cold room that seemed to press in around me.

I didn't delude myself that new meant anything akin to safe. I was just as much a sitting duck here as I had been at the last hospital.

26

The New Doctor

The new hospital meant a new doctor.

The New Doctor was a woman which should have made things easier. But somehow didn't. It didn't feel as though she made much of an effort to understand me. I felt like a number to her rather than a person. A box on her To Do list that needed to be checked off before she could go home to her nice house with its manicured front lawn, and 2.5 children and a husband that called her darling. Or maybe she lived alone, in an inner city apartment with a cat and a fridge full of wine. I had no way of knowing. I never would have had time to ask her.

The average amount of time I spent with her was always less than fifteen minutes. She would sit across from me in her chair, one leg crossed demurely over the other. She dressed in the kind of business clothes one buys from stores with glass doors. Her hair was always pulled back in a chic twisted bun, with a few strands left to fall artfully around her face.

'Ah yes, patient 23576b, nice to see you again,' she would say. 'How are you feeling about everything today?'

'Okay, I guess.' The truth was I didn't know how to feel. All the useful things I'd been doing with Mark and Rosemary had ended after the night in the room with the red mattress. If anything I felt empty.

She made a note on the page in the yellow file she had perched upon her lap. Had I even said anything noteworthy? I didn't think so.

'Could you expand on that?'

'Expand?' I played dumb. I didn't want to give her information she could use against me.

'Yes, expand. You know talk more about how you feel?'

I continued to stare blankly into her face. Polite but not really seeing her. Could I expand? There were a lot of things I didn't say to her.

Like, 'Doctor, my hips hurt and sometimes it's hard to walk. Doctor, do you think it's ironic to be raped in a hospital? Sorry Doctor, you didn't know I was raped? You mean it wasn't in the notes that came with me from the other hospital? Oh, they haven't sent the notes yet? How convenient. Doctor, do psychiatrists have to take the Hippocratic oath? No? Interesting. Why, is that interesting? Because I feel like you might benefit from having some kind of moral code governing your work. It doesn't have to be complicated, just a "I will not put patients on drugs that make them feel worse!" would be a nice start. Don't you think, Doctor?'

Somehow I didn't think she would have responded well to any of that. So I bit back my words. I kept them in the back of my throat. Or I swallowed them whole. They sat in the pit of my stomach. Churning around and blending together.

Sometimes, even now, I feel them, burning their way up to the back of my throat. Creating a big solid lump of pain and heartbreak, that makes it hard to breath.

But this was the price of getting out, I had to lock everything down, deep inside. I had to be fine. I couldn't afford to wear my wounds on full display. They had to be wrapped in bandages at all times and over the top of that I had to wear a thick coat of disguise.

This was the secret I learned from the New Doctor, that it didn't really matter how I felt. It all just came down to appearances.

'I mean I feel better, I guess.'

'That's good,' said the New Doctor, making another note in her file.

27

The Rat

Turning a surplus of attention in the direction of anyone is a dangerous game. Celebrities know this and deep down I think ordinary people know it as well. No one likes the idea of a stranger having complete access to their life. To be watched constantly is its own kind of hell. This chapter tells the story of my problem with the Rat. I do not know exactly when this problem began because I pretended even to myself for a good stretch of time that it was not happening. No one likes admitting they have a stalker, but when you are a mere mortal without the financial resources or closeted protection around you to deal with such a person, the prospect becomes all the more frightening. Add to this a house built in the 50s with easily pickable locks and parents who are blissfully unaware and the situation becomes ever dicier.

The first person I ever spoke to about the Rat was someone who came my way courtesy of Mr. Canberra. Let's call him Alec. I met Alec on my second week in the new hospital. The first thing I noticed about him were his shoes. They were the give away. The one flaw in an otherwise convincing disguise, a costume designed so he could pass as a nursing student. The shoes were military grade army boots. In our first conversation he told me he knew someone who flushed people down drains for a living.

He was sent by Mr. Canberra to scare me. I liked him instantly. Primarily because of how clean the ward became in his presence. He had that air of terrifying authority that made people behave better in his presence, like the school teacher who can silence a class with a look. We had many conversations, but on his last day of placement, a Friday, he brought up the subject of the Rat. He cut me off in the middle of what I thought was a very funny story.

'April, I don't want to talk about this. I want to know what you are going to do about the Rat.'

'The Rat?'

I didn't understand what he meant.

'The Rat that lives in your room, that creeps out at night and steals your treasures.'

I knew what he meant now. The Rat was my stalker. Alec had just confirmed it for me. All the signs were there. Stuff moving around my bedroom when I was out. Little bits of food missing from the fridge. A twisty uncomfortable feeling in the pit of my stomach as I was going to sleep at night. My house even provided the perfect hidey-hole for the Rat to crawl into. A room we called the cave that was used for storage and connected to my bedroom. You had to step down into the cave, so there was easily enough space to crawl from the cave into the empty space that made up the foundations of the house.

'I keep all my treasures up here now.' I placed a finger on my temple. This was something that I felt to be true, given everything I had been through, but my answer did not satisfy Alec.

'What happens when the Rat comes to nibble at your ear?' he asked me.

'I ask the Rat to stop.'

He grimaced as though he found my answer both childish and painful.

'This Rat will not stop, you could live on a dirt floor in Syria and this Rat would still find you.'

I nodded my head. I knew he was right.

'It is a very sick Rat.'

'Yes, it is. But what are you going to do about it?'

'Is your contract exclusive?' I asked him suddenly.

'There is no contract.'

'If there is no contract then why are you here? Don't tell me you're actually a nursing student!' I joked, trying to lighten the tone of the conversation.

He grimaced again, and looked at his feet.

'Let me guess,' I said slowly.

'I'd rather you didn't.'

'If there is no contract then I think it likely you went somewhere with a lot of sand.'

His face remained a mask.

'Yes, a beach of sorts.'

He smiled at this.

'You did some bad things on a sandy beach *somewhere* and because of this you are sent places to do awful things for awful people. Am I close?'

'Yes.'

'I have some money saved, I could pay to take care of my Rat problem for me? How much do you charge for your services?'

He shook his head. 'For you, I would do it for free, I could go now and be back within the hour.'

'How will you know it's my Rat?'

He grimaced again. 'Because he'll be hiding under your stairs waiting for you to get home.'

When I think back on it, the whole conversation feels surreal. Talking about killing someone as calmly as if it were the weather. I suppose the weeks in hospital had hardened me. Something in me knew I couldn't go through with it though. As much as having a Rat living under my stairs made me afraid to sleep at night.

'I can't let you do that.'

He looked at me incredulously, as though I was not fully comprehending the situation I was in.

'The Rat has just as much right to live as I do. If I ask you to take care of the Rat for me I'm no better than the man who sent you here. Promise me, you won't hurt the Rat.'

'And when the Rat hurts you?'

'Qué será, será,' I replied, almost meaning it.

28

Perhaps

When I got home, I worked diligently at the rat problem. I left him notes, all around my room. Please don't take my clothes. Please don't touch my clothes. Please don't come in at night. Please, if you must come in at night, don't touch me when I sleep. But my pleas fell on deaf ears. The Rat grew bolder. I would wake up from a dream with lipstick smeared across my face. This built to a crescendo one night when I heard a voice I cannot explain, as clear as day, right in my ear, instructing me to OPEN MY EYES NOW.

I saw the Rat above me, a needle clutched in his hand. I knew in that moment what he had been intending to do with it. I was seconds away from having a needle poked into my eye. I screamed at the Rat to get out. He ran for the door to my bathroom, which had a door that opened onto a path that ran down the side of the house. I chased after him.

Don't you fucking dare come back, I screamed into the dark of the suburban street as I watched him run.

I suspect something was done about the Rat. What that was exactly I am not sure. But it's been years since I've seen him. Part of me is glad for the weight that now cloaks my body, as though if I become desirable again I will draw the

Rat out of hiding, back to live under my floorboards again.

My small uninteresting life does little to tempt the Rat or provoke Mr. Canberra, but I know that there is a distinct possibility that publishing this book will mean I meet one or both of them again. Maya Angelou wrote that 'There is no greater agony than bearing an untold story inside you.' I know her words to be true because I have lived them. For seven years this story has sat alone in a quiet box in my head. To bring it into the light, to stand in the sun with it, is a risk. A risk that if you're reading this I have taken, on a foolish whim or from a deep bolt of courage, I know not yet. To illustrate this risk I will share the story of my final meeting with Alec, because it may convince you of the lengths that Mr. Canberra was prepared to go to make sure that this story did not leave my lips.

The next and last time I saw Alec was the night after our conversation about the Rat.

I was still in hospital at this point and almost asleep, when I felt a cold raindrop press against my forehead. That's weird, I thought, it doesn't rain indoors.

I opened my eyes.

Alec was standing above me with a gun pressed into my head.

I didn't know what to say. There wasn't time to be scared exactly. Instantly, my mental list of the faces of people I loved came back to the surface. I closed my eyes. I waited. One one thousand. Two one thousand. I mentally scanned through the gallery again. Still nothing happened. Maybe this is what death feels like? Maybe I'm already bleeding out, and my brain hasn't processed it yet, because there's a bullet lodged in it.

Above me Alec laughed. Okay, I'm not dead yet. Why did he laugh? Does he find killing people amusing? Maybe he's more suited to his job than I thought.

'I'm not going to kill you, April.'

Oh, said my brain. Well, that's a relief. I opened my eyes. 'What's the gun for then?' I asked, trying to keep the fear out my voice.

'It's a prop, really,' said Alec, moving it away from my head.

'You mean it's fake?'

'No, it's very much a real gun.'

'How is it a prop then?'

'It's a prop because I brought it in here to scare you. Not to kill you.'

I looked at him skeptically.

'Here,' he said 'I'll put it down on this chair over there if you don't believe me.' He crossed the room in two strides and placed the gun on the chair.

'Why are you here if you're not going to hurt me?' Even with the gun across the room, I still didn't entirely believe him. It felt too good to be true, cheating death for the second time in two weeks.

'Ah, that. Well, Mr. Canberra made me come.'

As he said Mr. Canberra's name I felt my face tighten. For the first time, I felt real fear returning to my system. Maybe it was a delayed reaction. Or maybe, said another voice, you're not scared of Alec, just of Mr. Canberra.

'Yeah, you remember him huh?' said Alec, reading the expression on my face. 'He really did a number on you didn't he? He showed me the photo you know. It was awful. I mean really sick, your arm and your leg twisted up like that. I had to pretend to enjoy it. Anyway, yeah he wants me to make a little video with you.'

'What kind of video?' I asked. I knew Alec didn't want to hurt me, but I didn't doubt that he could.

'It's really unimaginative. Quite boring actually. He wants

me to hold a gun to your head, and tell you that if you ever go to the police or the media, he'll kill you. And he wants you to cry. And promise that you won't do those things. That's it. Like I said, pretty boring.'

The way he said it I almost laughed. I didn't feel remotely like crying. The whole situation was just funny to me now. I smiled at Alec then. 'He sent you here for a whole week just to say that?' I asked.

'Essentially, yes. Do you think you can do it? Cry I mean?'

'If I don't get it the first time, we can always do just another take, right?' I joked lamely.

'True,' he said, crossing the room again and picking up the gun. He pulled out an old flip phone from his pocket. It was so old, that I was surprised it could even take a video. He pressed the gun to my head again.

'You going to call action?' I joked again. I didn't know why I'd suddenly turned into such a comedian but the situation was so weird that I couldn't help but see the humour in it. Here was Alec, a trained killer, still dressed in his student nurse disguise, holding a gun and filming me on a flip phone and I was meant to be scared?

Maybe I would have been terrified doing this with a stranger who appeared out of the blue.

But with Alec? I knew Alec. He was a good person and somehow in the most bizarre way I just felt safe.

He recited his lines. I tried to remember what it was like to be really afraid. I wished for those eye drops actors use to cry on cue. Somehow I managed to make a single tear roll down my cheek.

When he put the phone down I continued with my lame joke, 'Do we need another take?' I asked.

He shook his head, packed the gun neatly away into his belt and started for the door.

'Wait,' I called after him. 'Do you think I'll ever see you

again?'

'Perhaps,' he replied with a smile.

29

A Sort of Freedom

A week after Alec's visit to my room, I was sent home from the hospital. Coming home after so long should have felt like a victory but instead I felt slightly crippled. I was very numb. I had no experience living through anything like this. It was as though I was finally sitting down after a long time on my feet. I had no willpower left to get back up again. So I became kind of frozen. Existing was my only goal.

I neglected even the most basic of tasks. There were days when the only thing I achieved was to get up a little before dinner time. I got dressed and sat at the table with my parents for the evening meal. Feeling too hollow even to make an attempt at conversation.

It's not a pretty picture. It's not the kind of neat 'tie everything in a bow' ending that a novel needs. But the reality was that I had been well and truly broken. It would take considerable time and effort before I felt any semblance of okay again. It happened though. Gradually. Painfully.

I went back to university and to my job. My days consisted of more things again. I had assignments, reading, textbooks and notes. I even had people I spoke to about their weekend or the weather that day. In some ways I seemed healed. In others, I remained desperately broken.

To a large degree my brain skirted around thinking about what I'd been through. I began to feel disconnected from it. The same way you forget the floor plan to your old high school after a few years of no longer attending. There were details of what I'd been through that began to feel distant and alien even to me. Things that became blurred or fuzzy around the edges.

Maybe it was some combination of this fuzziness and a desire to squash everything down that led me to pick at my invisible wounds. To prod and poke at them, trying to see if they still hurt. This is what led me to Tinder. It was a sort of game. How far can I push myself into uncomfortable situations without anyone noticing my trauma. Look how okay I am, I can have sex and it doesn't even have to mean anything.

Looking back on it now, it feels stupid. And manipulative. But I did it over and over for months and months. I ripped off the bandaids I'd stuck to my invisible wounds just to see if they would bleed. And bleed they did.

It would always be fine up until a point. Then my body would flick a switch and I wanted to be out of that room as fast as possible. Most of the time, the guys I was with pretended not to notice. We would never see or message each other again. That was the procedure.

One night, I was sitting on my bed with a boy who under other circumstances I would have really liked.

He turned to me with a serious expression on his face. 'I think I can ask this considering everything we just did.'

'Okay,' I replied.

'Okay, I'm just going to say it, then. Were you… were you raped?'

'Why would you ask that?' I asked, faking a puzzled expression.

'I don't know. It's just a feeling I got.'

What was I supposed to say? More than likely I was never going to see this boy again. Was I just supposed to spill the entire story out onto the floor, just to confirm his superstition? Did he really want that? I decided in that moment just to lie. 'I mean, yes, something happened but it wasn't that.'

'Really? Good. I'm glad, not that something happened, but that you weren't you know…'

'Yeah. Me too,' I replied softly.

I thought a lot about that night while writing this story. About why I couldn't just be honest with him. Part of me sometimes wants to turn off every empathetic part of me. To turn away and to pretend I do not see that it happens to other people too.

Part of me wants to be a man, to be able to say I would never do that, and no one I know would ever do that, so it must not be as big a problem as other people make it out to be. It's like a faraway abstract problem, like hunger in the third world.

And then another part of me says if you lose the ability to feel this, where does it stop? Do you lose the ability to have any empathic capability at all? Because you feel this more than you feel a lot of other things. It takes up a hell of a lot of space inside of you. What are you going to fill it with, wires and cables?

I couldn't really answer this at first. But after a while I found something that helped. I tried to say April, that pain, you hold onto it because it's the best part of you.

It's the bravest part.

30

The Girl in the Lilac Dress

I am walking on a road towards a cliff. It is a cliff I will one day reach, and then I must find the courage to jump off. Into what I do not know. Nor do I wish to speculate too long on it. I cannot change my route and walk in a different direction. I can sit on the ground and go nowhere. I could if I wanted spend the rest of my life sitting on the ground. It would be a peaceful, uncomplicated life, but not a happy one. The bile of regret would burn holes in my chest. My legs would stiffen from being held in the same position. Jumping from the cliff is honest. The girl who jumps does not live in fear. Nor is she ignorant of the consequences. She knows jumping from the cliff may be the last important thing she does. Once I told a friend that I hated that falling felt like flying til the bone crush. Does falling feel like flying? Perhaps it will not be a fall. Perhaps it will be a hole that opens in my chest. Perhaps the edge of a blade.

Once, twice already in this story I was ready to die. That courage, the readiness I felt, as though everything was put away in order has long since faded. I am once again afraid. Afraid of the cliff I know is coming. But fear is not the only thing I feel. There is hope too. It mingles with fear until I am in a mess of feelings. Unable to think. To write clearly. This is the last chapter of my story. My memoir. And so I guess it is appropriate I am thinking about closure. About endings.

For a long time closure has felt like pixie dust to me. Scattered in the tiniest of quantities by an unreliable fairy. In my mind, this fairy clocks in late, leaves early and chooses who gets closure in a completely haphazard way. Perhaps she throws a dart at a board and decides you get over your ex-girlfriend six years after the relationship ended.

It has been seven years since the events of this story took place. Seven years, as others have gotten on with their lives, I have searched for the Closure Fairy. I've wrestled with what it means to be a good survivor. As though there is some clear instruction manual, some completely obvious set of rules you can apply when you are raped. I've learnt that there is no right or wrong. There are only choices.

Silence has been my friend a long time now. To speak is opening the curtains in a room that has always been dark. I may wish to snatch back these words.

Sometimes I pray to be a blank slate. Clean canvas with fresh brushes. It would be nice to see an untarnished thing in the mirror again. To feel painting was ahead of me. That all the marks on my canvas have been my choice.

Part of my heart wanted to be dancing around a rotunda in a lilac dress, rain pouring down, hope shining in my eyes. But I couldn't put on the lilac dress. So I left her there.

Sometimes I visit her. I go back to the grave of the girl I used to be.

I don't find it lined with flowers.

I couldn't write an inscription on the headstone either.

Survivor is too bold a word.

Fearless feels too hopeful.

Brave too much to live up to.

Innocent.

That's what I wrote.
And then I let her go back to dancing.

31

This Book Wouldn't Exist Without You

In mid 2018, I held a copy of this book in my hands before ever having written a word of it. I can't explain how that was possible as I fear it would get some people in quite significant trouble. That same night, I was asked to give a speech accepting an award for work I had not yet done. I was a little drunk, so I can't remember if that speech was filmed or not. I hope it was not, as I did a very bad job of it.

See, at the time, I thought I was going skip writing this book altogether and just write a film script. In my incredibly terrible acceptance speech, I think I only thanked two people which when I think about it now, seems absurd, but in my defence I'm pretty sure my pretend (?) acceptance speech was for one of those nasty award shows that like playing music to kick people off stage.

Anyway, suffice to say this time I want to do it right.

So, ummm… Where do I start?

To the people who should be here included but won't be.

Simply, thank you.

Dad, for every day I gave you chapters without proofreading them at all. For every: typo, tense slip, repeated word, spelling mistake, sentence that didn't actually make sense, and uncurly apostrophe, that you corrected. Thank you. I wouldn't have gotten here without you. If I get the chance to write something else, I'll try not to abuse your editing services quite as much. Also, I love you.

Mum, I love you and I hope you never read this.

Nerida, for listening to me with unwavering empathy.

Mark, for standing with me through awful moments.

Edward, Yeah, just Edward. I don't feel the need to explain that one.

Eugene, for painting me in the only reflection I really ever truly liked.

Taylor, there were many days writing this novel I felt I would never get here. Sometimes the only thing that kept me going was the faith you had already placed in me. I can never capture what it meant to me that when I turned up on the doorstep of your castle, a castle, you had built stone by stone, by hand, that you not only opened the front gates to me, but also every door, room and secret passage way.

When I got excited and pulled out a paintbrush and a palette of watercolours from my pocket, asking to paint a wall, you gave me your blessing. Then after I'd done the best I could with my watercolours, you returned to my wall with your own brush and turned it into a tapestry with a kind of beauty and magic I could never have imagined.

Publishing this book is a risk, and because it feels foolish to make a will at twenty-seven with no assets to speak of, Taylor, for the record, if they ever consider April's story worthy of an adaption, I'd want you to make it.

Having said that, this is a work of fiction. Any resemblance to real people or events is entirely co-incidental!

However, to anyone who recognises themselves in this story, I hope you can understand why I needed to write it.

Milton Keynes UK
Ingram Content Group UK Ltd.
UKHW021028280324
440296UK00006B/70